This book b

Margaret Fitzgerald 1994

Children's
POOLBEG

First published by J.M. Dent & Sons Ltd, 1960
This edition 1990 by
Poolbeg Press Ltd,
A Division of Poolbeg Enterprises Ltd,
Knocksedan House,
Swords, Co Dublin, Ireland.
Reprinted 1993

ISBN 1 85371 070 9

Cover design by Judith O'Dwyer,
Printed by The Guernsey Press Ltd,
Vale, Guernsey, Channel Islands.

SALLY FROM CORK

SALLY FROM CORK

PATRICIA LYNCH

Children's
POOLBEG

Contents

1
On Wise's Hill

ally Nolan sat half-way down the steep stone steps in front of one of the tall old houses at the bottom of Wise's Hill in Cork city. The River Lee flowed below on its way to the great harbour. She could see steamships starting on their voyages, returning home from upstream and down.

Herds of cows trotted by; men and women swarmed out of shops and offices; children ran, hopped, sauntered, and gathered about the apple-women who were packing up their half-empty baskets.

One woman, as she passed, tossed an apple to Sally. The little girl caught it neatly and sank her teeth through the thin red skin. The sharp juice spurted on her face and she crunched the crisp fruit slowly.

Sally leaned against a bulging brown canvas bag. She was wearing her best frock and coat, the red tammy Mrs Mooney had knitted for her last birthday, and her new laced boots, good strong boys' boots guaranteed to keep out wet and stand up to the cobbles and hills of Cork.

"Horrid old boots!" said Sally, kicking a stone down the hill.

With shouts and the clatter of their iron-shod footwear, men were pushing trucks and rolling barrels along the quays. Loaded lorries thundered over Patrick's Bridge.

She looked up to where the houses at the bend seemed to be bowing to each other across the street then down to where the ships lay at anchor, dark and silent, while others, blazing with lights, surged out of sight, with the smooth purr of their engines growing fainter as they went.

"It could be fun waiting here for me sister and me brother to take me away with them all the way to England," Sally told herself. "But only if I didn't have to wait alone, with me friends inside packing to go to America. I should be going with them by rights!"

She swallowed the last bit of apple, pushed back her tumbled brown hair neatly under the soft red tammy which closely framed her thin, anxious little face, and sat up straight.

"Didn't I promise to be brave," she murmured. "And this is the time for it!"

The door behind her opened and Mrs Mooney looked out.

"Come along in, girleen!" she called. "Let's drink the last cup of tay together!"

Sally's big solemn brown eyes looked back at the short, stout, worried little woman with the thin plait of fair hair fastened round her head, Der and Des, the youngest of the Mooneys, clutching her skirt as if they feared she would run away from them.

"I daren't!" answered Sally. "Suppose me sister Kitty and me brother Dominick went by and, not seeing me waiting on them, travelled straight back to England without me. Then I would be in a fix!"

She sniffed a little to choke back her tears. The two fat little boys in their new blue suits rushed out to her and crouched down, one on each side, wailing their loudest.

"If I'm not the misfortunate woman!" sighed Mrs Mooney. "Come in out of that, ye two tormints, and ate the last dacent meal ye'll be having in this country. Sally, darling, don't be vexing me this last day we're together! Let ye come in now!"

"If Sally isn't coming to Americy, I'm not coming neither," declared Des.

"Nor me too!" added Der, who always agreed with his brother.

Janey, the eldest of the young Mooneys, propped herself against the door, her arms folded.

"The lads have started eating," she announced, "and me da says if some haven't sense enough to come in when there's food, he'll not stop them that have."

She gave a giggle.

"He's raging mad! He says if all of you don't stop ullagoning, it's Australia he'll make for and let his brother Chris put up with us in America. As if it's our fault poor little Sally isn't coming too! Sure we can't help fretting!"

"Come in, pet," coaxed Mrs Mooney. "Let's all part in friendship. And listen now! The minit we get over to Americy I'll start axing and watching for yor da. Sure ye haven't forgotten him, the poor chap, though tis ages since he went and not a line from him, not a word. If he's there I'll track him down and tell him the whole sad story. He'll be shook when he hears yer poor mother's gone and his three misfortunate childer are left to face the world on their own."

"Ah, Mammy! What ails ye?" protested

Janey. "You're making poor Sally cry! Leave her alone!"

"Ye're right, Janey, dead right!" agreed Mrs Mooney. "Don't mind me, Sally! I'm all moidhered at going away and I don't rightly know what I'm after saying! This I do promise. We'll start saving the minit we set foot in the great United States of Americy. This time next year we may be millionaires and tisn't the bit of a fare will stop us travelling over to fetch ye. We might fly the journey!"

She stopped breathlessly, a little frightened at her own daring.

"Pigs might fly!" said Janey. "So why not the Mooneys? I'm going in while there's a sup of tea left."

She went in. Mrs Mooney followed.

"To please me, go in!" Sally told Des and Der. "And do stop that horrid noise or I'll never speak to you again!"

"The teapot's empty!" called Janey Mooney.

Der and Des sniffed, scrambled to their feet and ran in. At the door they looked back.

Sally was gazing down towards the river.

"Already she has forgotten us," they thought sadly.

They were wrong. Sally would never forget the Mooneys.

Three years ago Sally and her brother Dominick had been left alone in the world. He was two years younger and her age now was twelve years and eight months.

The only relation they knew was their sister Kitty who was working in London. Mr Mooney wrote to her saying that his wife would take care of the children until she came to fetch them.

She didn't come but sent the money for one half-fare.

"I can't manage two," she wrote. "So perhaps you had better send the boy. I know we have rich relations in America but I've mislaid their address and when I sent them a letter after me mother died, they didn't answer."

So the Mooneys had taken Sally down to the boat to see the last of her brother. He looked very small as he stood by the rail, clutching a brown-paper parcel and wearing a coat far too big for him.

Yet he smiled as he waved, for he was excited at the prospect of a voyage. But Mrs Mooney had assured him they wouldn't be parted for long.

"You can do the messages and mind the young ones when you're home from school," she told Sally. "Ye're such a scrap we won't miss the bit and sup. When I cut down one of the frocks me cousin sends me from Americy, there'll be plenty to run up a dress for ye as well as for Janey! Tis the boots cost money. Still, we'll manage!"

A card came from their American cousins at Easter and a present at Christmas.

Janey, the oldest of the young Mooneys, helped Sally to write letters to her sister in London though they were never answered. Janey wrote all the letters for the family and some for neighbours. Her parents were very proud of her and she was proud of herself.

Yet Janey wasn't happy. Why should Sally be left behind? What would she do without them? Janey didn't say a word about it. Where was the use in upsetting herself or Sally, or her mother? One day Sally would join them. She was sure of that!

At night Sally dreamed of her brother over the sea in a big strange city. Now she would soon be with him—and her sister Kitty.

What was Kitty like? Would she have red hair, as untidy as Mrs Mooney's? Would she be as pale and severe as the woman at the corner shop? Or big and jolly? And Dom, her little brother—would he remember her? Would she remember him?

A black car, sitting on the sill of an open window just above Sally's head, jumped down and curled up beside her. Sally stroked its long thick fur, from the pointed ears to the bushy tail.

She had often wished Sooty belonged to her. Now she was glad he could stay peacefully in Cork. He mightn't be a good traveller. And his owner, old Mrs Leary, was good to him. There she was now, coming up the hill from her pitch on Pope's Quay, the empty apple basket swinging on her arm.

Sooty jumped down and trotted, miaowing, to meet her.

"So ye're still here, pet?" said Mrs Leary to Sally. "I saved an apple, a gorgeous pippin for ye. Then I thought ye'd be gone, so I sold it to the young one from the paper shop. Now I wish I hadn't been in such a desprit hurry!"

"Thank you all the same," returned Sally politely.

"Someone else gave me one—a big red apple."

"Are ye lonesome at the thought of foreign parts?" asked Mrs Leary sympathetically.

Sally nodded.

"Don't fret!" advised the old woman. "Tisn't as if ye were going to Mericay. London isn't all that far, and ye're young. Besides, aren't yer brother and yer sister coming to fetch ye? Tis sad to be leaving yer own country. Yet tis grand to be with the ones ye rightly belong to. Remember that!"

Sally nodded again.

"Here's old Paudeen O'Donnell and his dog Usheen!" exclaimed Mrs Leary. "Will ye look at the walk of him strutting along as if he were a king, and that villyan of a dog of his that has poor Sooty heart-scalded!"

"He sings lovely ballads," protested Sally. "And Usheen won't torment Sooty while I'm here!"

"Ah, well!" sighed Mrs Leary, folding her arms, while Sooty's thick black fur stood up stiffly and his tail fiercely lashed his sides.

"How's yerself, Mrs Leary?" asked the ballad singer, coming to a stop before the group on the steps and raising his battered old felt hat with a flourish. "And how's the young emigrant, God help her!"

"Grand, Paudeen, grand!" replied Mrs Leary, looking very severely at the terrier, who stood still, his ears cocked and his stump of a tail wagging almost as furiously as Sooty's.

"I'm very well, thank you, Mr O'Donnell!" answered Sally, stroking the cat. "And I'm not an emigrant yet," she added.

The old man laughed.

"That's the style! Keep a brave heart and ye'll never be daunted. Now why are ye frowning at me poor dog? Is it taking that thief of a cat's part ye are? Sure, ye've no sense!"

"Me cat, Sooty, isn't a thief and well ye know it, Paudeen O'Donnell," exclaimed the apple seller. "Ye should be ashamed to set dumb animals at one another."

"Sure I wouldn't do that," protested Paudeen, giving his dog a slap. "Sit down now, ye ruffian, and be a credit to the hill."

Usheen obeyed and lay panting. The cat gazed at her enemy with half-closed eyes.

"When are ye leaving us, child?" asked the old man.

"As soon as me sister and me brother come for me," answered Sally. "I don't know what's keeping them."

"I'll be down at the boat to see the last of ye!" promised Paudeen. "Come along, Usheen, me lad, I'm starving for a sup of tay!"

He strode up the hill, the dog barking at his heels to show defiance. Mrs Leary rose.

"I'll keep a watch out," she said. "I'll not say goodbye till the last minit!"

Mr Mooney came to the door.

"Come in out of that, ye young eejit!" he

ordered. "I've poured a cup of tay for ye and there's a slice of toast. Tis the last chance ye'll have to be sharing a meal wid the Mooneys, so don't miss it!"

"Thank you, Mr Mooney!" said Sally.

She half rose, then sat down again, for a sturdy boy with dark hair blowing back from his round red face came running up the hill and, behind him, as lightly as if she were carried by the wind, came an elegant young woman who pulled the boy back as he was passing Sally.

"Don't you know your own sister?" she asked.

2
Goodbye, Cork!

uddenly everyone in the tall old house was out on the steps.

"Ye haven't altered, barring the height and width of ye, since the day ye went off roaring and screaming at parting from yer poor little sister," Mrs Mooney told the boy. "Now come in the two of ye and I'll boil up the kettle."

"We can't stop!" declared the young woman. "We're not going back on the ship we came in. There's one off in half an hour and they'll not wait a minute for us. Sally, darling! How you've grown! Not so much as Dom though. He's bigger than you are. Dom, kiss your little sister!"

She hugged Sally and Sally hugged her. They hadn't set eyes on one another since Sally was very, very young—three years ago. But she liked her sister at once. She liked her brother too, though the great smacking kiss he gave her almost took her breath away.

"You're Mrs Mooney!" Kitty said to the little red-haired woman. "How can I thank you for all your kindness to Sally? And you must be Mr Mooney!"

She turned to him. The Mooneys crowded round. Janey ran out to see Sally's sister. The two boys gobbled the last bits of toast and rushed out too.

"We'll come down and see the three of yez off!" declared Mr Mooney. "We'd as well get used to ships, for we'll be starting ourselves tomorrow. One of you lads take Sally's bag. Tis the last ye'll be able to do for her!"

The neighbours swarmed from the houses on each side to say goodbye and to give Sally a send-off. She found herself clutching a bag of sweets. Mr Mooney took the canvas bag from her and handed it to Janey, who passed it to the boys.

"Carry that!" she ordered. "And carry it properly!"

"I brought this bit of a shawl!" gasped Mrs Mooney. "The child may be glad of it in that terrible city. And I popped in all the bits and pieces the neighbours brought for her. She'll need them, so she will, the poor scrap!"

"Aren't we leaving home too? Aren't we emigrants?" demanded Mr Mooney. "Just because we're not skinny little girls wid big eyes and hair falling into them, nobody cares!"

The ballad singer led the way. When he began to sing "The Emigrant's Farewell" the neighbours formed into a procession, and the fiddler from up the hill came hurrying along at the tail, playing so well he was astonished at himself.

"Some great man might hear me," he thought, "and, who knows, if a letter mightn't come one day axing me over to London or New York itself."

Kitty Nolan, Sally's sister, marched between Sally and Dominick. At first she was very bewildered. This wasn't the way people used to leave home. She remembered her mother's tears, her father's sorrow and the wailing of other parents whose children were going from them, perhaps for ever.

Dominick glanced at his new, strange sister. Her face was flushed, her eyes sparkled and she tramped along in her heavy boys' boots as if she were leading an army.

"They must like her an awful lot!" he reflected.

He hadn't been too sure that he wanted a

young sister over in London. He knew Kitty had been dismayed when she realized that Sally hadn't another relation in the world who would care for her.

"Haven't I done enough in taking Dom?" she had asked herself. "How can I manage to keep two children as well as myself?"

Now, as the haunting strains of

I'm sitting on the stile, Mary,
Where we sat side by side

rose about her, she clutched Sally's hand and smiled down at her.

"I'll do my best to make you happy," she said.

They marched along; the quays were quieter now. People were mostly indoors having the pleasantest meal of the day. Those still on the way home stood on kerb and doorstep to watch the higgledy-piggledy procession. A few clapped, others joined in, singing and marching in time to the music.

"Tisn't many young ones has this kind of a send-off and they leaving home and country behind," sighed Mrs Mooney. "They'll not be doing this for us tomorrow."

The turf man, who had hurried down at the last moment, leaving his donkey resting after a hard day's work, trundled his empty cart. The apple-woman had taken off her apron and felt she was no disgrace to such a grand company.

"They never did this for me!" thought Dominick. "There must be something special about Sally!"

He began to feel proud of his sister.

"Here we are!" cried Kitty suddenly.

The ballad singer halted.

"*Wave of Tory*," he chanted.

That was the name painted in faded gold on the stern of a small steamer moored below Patrick's Bridge.

The steamer was so dingy and untidy it looked like a tinker's boat among the trim smart steamers moored alongside. Two men in their shirt-sleeves, Captain MacCarthy, and the mate, Jim Brady, with caps stuck at the backs of their heads, leaned over the side, smoking.

The crews of the boards on each side stared wondering and excited at the procession.

The captain of the *Wave of Tory* saluted Kitty.

"Didn't know you were such a famous young woman in your own place!" he said. "Sorry there isn't time to make a speech. We must be off at once! We were waiting on you!"

"Tisn't for me!" explained Kitty. "It's for Sally here!"

Mr Mooney gave a cheer which was taken up

by the crowd. He swung Sally down to the deck before Mrs Mooney had a chance even to hug her.

The captain pulled Kitty after Sally. Dominick scrambled on board without help and they stood in a row, smiling and waving. At the last moment Sally's bag was pushed after her along with a heap of presents which had been almost forgotten.

The ballad singer began "Come Back to Erin." The fiddler made as much noise as he could and Sally gazed back at her friends, wondering why they were growing smaller and more distant, until a big friendly woman, in a flowered overall, drew her back from the side.

"Come below, pet!" she said. "And have a sup of tay. Tis grand to have that number of friends, only ye don't want to spend too long on goodbyes. Tis sad they are at the best of times."

They crowded down into a small cabin, unexpectedly bright and cosy after the dingy deck, with a cloth crooked yet clean, and with shining knives and forks heaped in the centre where, at the table, Sally ate her first meal on board ship.

Blackrock Castle, Spike Island, even Cobh, where the passengers came on shore from the great American liners, were passed unnoticed.

3
On the Ocean Wave

"I never properly said goodbye!" murmured Sally.

She opened her eyes and gazed about the tiny cabin.

Her coat, hanging on the back of the door, swayed to and fro. The canvas bag which held her clothes, her six books—*Robinson Crusoe*, *Hans Andersen's Fairy Tales*, *Grimms' Fairy Tales*, *Irish History*, a *Treasury of Irish Poems* and a battered old copy of *Oliver Twist* with many strange black-and-white pictures, slid across the strip of tattered carpet.

The piece of pink soap which Janey had given her slipped from its shallow nest behind the wash-basin and lay over the hole where the water ran out. Her brush and comb tumbled from the narrow glass shelf above and settled beside the soap.

Those boys' strong boots, which Sally so disliked, wandered from the tiny settee to the bunks and back again as if trying to dance.

"And me wanting to be the best dancer in the school," thought Sally mournfully. "I was just like an elephant in the zoo hopping around!"

Her sister's shining high-heeled shoes were sliding about too, but daintily, gracefully. Her coat and dress were neatly folded on the settee. As Sally watched they moved slowly, gently to the edge and dropped in a heap on top of the shoes and there they lay, heaving and wriggling.

Sally had once been on an excursion in a steamer which went from Patrick's Bridge down the Lee, round Spike Island and back again. It had been a warm sunny day, and though they all sang and danced Sally had been disappointed. The journey would have been just as exciting if they had gone by bus, though that was not possible.

The *Wave of Tory* was behaving just as Sally thought a ship should behave. It was going up and down, up and down. She could hear the waves beating against the sides as she expected them to.

Yet she wasn't satisfied. She felt uneasy and

a little bit frightened.

She raised herself in the bunk.

Right beside her was a thick round glass window. She knew it was called a porthole and felt pleased at her knowledge.

Suddenly she stared and, gazing into the curve of a green foam-crested wave, opened her mouth to scream. Then, remembering her promise to be brave, closed it again.

"Is the ship going down?" she wondered, shivering and longing for Mrs Mooney's comforting smile. Mrs Mooney was never afraid of anything.

The wave broke and another surged into its place. The ship shook and staggered but kept on. Shoes and clothes careered over the floor. Sally's coat swung, her canvas bag bumped its way around.

"We're still on top of the sea and no one's shouting or screaming, so everything must be all right," decided Sally, determined to be brave.

She snuggled luxuriously against her pillow. In the bunk below was the sister she had almost forgotten and was only beginning to know.

Now it was the Mooneys who seemed strange and far away.

There was a bang on the door.

A voice, with a comforting Cork accent, said "Excuse me!" and the door opened.

There entered the big dark woman who had welcomed them on board the evening before. She wore a white apron on top of her overall and she carried a loaded tray. Peeping under her arm was Dominick's brown face, brown eyes friendly and inquiring.

Sally knew she should say "Good morning, Mrs Regan! I hope you slept well!" Only she was too amazed to do anything but stare.

Her mouth began to water and no wonder.

There was a dish of hot buttered toast, another of fried eggs, crisp curls of bacon and brown, bursting sausages, not to mind a brown steaming teapot and a plate of twisted rolls.

Sally also saw a saucer of little pats of butter and a glass dish of jam. She thought it was strawberry.

"Sit there, lad!" said the woman, nodding towards the settee with the long mirror at the back.

The boy obeyed. The tray was fixed across the wash-basin. Mrs Regan stood with her hands on her hips, smiling down at Kitty, who was still sound asleep.

"Isn't it wonderful to be able to sleep that way!" she chuckled. "Look at the happy face of that one! Sure she's having such a grand dream tis a pity to wake her. Still and all, the breakfast mustn't spoil and, sure, there's a night at the end of every day."

"She's opening her eyes!" cried Dominick. "Kitty, it's your breakfast. Wake up! Wake up! Breakfast in your bunk!"

Sally leaned over and saw her sister sitting up.

"How lovely!" cried the older girl. "I haven't had breakfast in bed for years! Mrs Regan, you're a darling!"

Sally had never had breakfast in bed before. On Wise's Hill one had to be very, very young, old or ill to have breakfast in bed.

"Of course," she reflected, "a bunk isn't a real bed. All the same it's lovely to sit up and have breakfast without washing or dressing. I think I'd like to sleep in a bunk always."

Breakfast with the Mooneys had been a hurried business of strong, stewed tea, soda bread and farmer's butter and, for Mr Mooney, a boiled egg.

Kitty sat up smiling. She was even more pleased than Sally to be having her breakfast in bed.

"How kind you are!" she said to Mrs Regan. "I have never had breakfast in bed on a ship before, not even coming over on *The Giant's Causeway*!"

"That's a smart little ship and a grand captain to mind it," declared Mrs Regan. "I never saw a cleaner, brighter ship in me life. But for comfort and good aiting ye can't beat the *Wave of Tory*. What the others spend on paint and soap we spend on food and drink.

"After all, ye can't pass the day looking at the ship ye're living in. And when there's a storm we ride high and dry, while *The Giant's Causeway*, and ships far bigger, flounder along like a herd of rhinoceroses.

"To crown all, we're making a record run. The Captain, God help him, says he's never known anything like it. We're saving hours! Even if we're held up in the Thames we'll not be hindered when all's said and done. So we're all very aisy in ourselves!"

Kitty nodded. Her mouth was too full of toast and sausage for her to speak.

Dominick didn't mind talking with his mouth full.

"Even the steward was feeling queer on *The Giant's Causeway*," he told Mrs Regan.

The fat woman roared with laughter.

"Tis a good thing he can't hear you give out that class of talk!" she told the boy, pouring herself another cup of tea and eating two slices of toast put together.

"Sure the poor man isn't like me. I know him well and he has no appetite at all. Sure, ye'd pity him! I've had one good breakfast but I'm as hungry as if I hadn't looked at food for a week.

"Cast yer eye at that child, cocked up there, listening wid her ears wide open. Ah, Kitty allanna! Tis terrible the way the young is leaving their own country. Still, she'll be great company for you and the lad!

"Ye might bring the tray back to the galley when ye're up and dressed. I have to help the cook. That's the class of ship this is!"

Kitty emptied the teapot, ate every bit of toast and didn't even leave a rind of bacon.

Dominick piled the cups, saucers and plates on the tray, opened the door carefully and squeezed out.

"Dom is a great boy!" said Kitty. "This is the first real holiday we've had since we went to England and it's wonderful. Breakfast in bed is a real treat when you have to be up every morning at six. You can wash first. I'm going to stay in bed as long as I can!"

Sally clambered down to the floor.

"Don't rich people have breakfast in bed in England?" she asked, looking very puzzled.

Kitty laughed.

"I expect some of them do. Only I'm not rich. Did you think I was?"

"Mrs Mooney said you must have a mint of money to be able to come over and bring Dominick with you, just to fetch me."

Kitty looked so serious Sally felt anxious. Had she been very rude?

"I'm sorry!" she murmured. "I shouldn't have said that. I'm terribly glad you both did come. I was feeling so lonely. I was afraid perhaps you wouldn't come, that you didn't want me!"

Kitty's big hazel eyes filled with tears.

"Poor little Sally!" she cried. "I've wanted to have you with me just as much as I wanted Dominick. Only when he came over I just had enough money to pay one half-fare. Since then I've been saving up, hoping we'd be able to come back one day."

She sighed and sat so still Sally would have thought her asleep only that her eyes were wide open, gazing far away.

Suddenly she turned and smiled.

"It was lucky I did save up. We were able to have this journey, and, when we do go back, the three of us will be together."

"I'm very glad not to be alone in the world any more," said Sally.

"Weren't the Mooneys good to you?" asked Kitty sorrowfully.

"Oh, they were! They were! Only I knew I didn't belong to them. It's wonderful to have a sister and a brother too. You can't imagine!"

Kitty nodded.

"I can! I promised mother I'd take care of you and Dom. I did my best but I wasn't very old and when Mrs Mooney offered to keep you because you could help with the children, the cooking and the cleaning, I thought it was a wonderful chance. I never dreamed I'd have to leave you there so long.

"I had to take Dom. He was so little and nobody else wanted him. Now he's as big or bigger than you are and he's grown into a fine lad. I couldn't manage without him."

4
Fog in the Channel

ally was feeling very adventurous when, at last, she opened the cabin door and stepped outside. The narrow passage was dark and there were so many strange sounds she wondered which way she should go.

Men were shouting and stamping; horns were sounding, shrill or hoarse; a mournful voice was singing. Far away and under, over, through all the other sounds, the sea beat steadily against the little ship.

"It's all wonderful," she thought. "As well as being a traveller, I've the nicest sister and brother in the world! I'm sure they are!"

"Ahoy there!" called a friendly voice. "Come on deck and see the sights!"

There were steep steps rising up at the end of

the passage. Sally ran towards them, swaying from side to side against the walls, for she was quite unused to the motion of the boat. Then she climbed up, clinging to the handrails at each side.

When she reached the top Sally stood still, startled and confused, for she stepped into a mist so thick she could scarcely see a foot before her.

A laughing face came close and a warm hand grasped hers.

"Oh, Dom!" she cried. "Isn't this all very strange?"

"It's wonderful!" declared the boy. "Just listen!"

They stood, hearing from every side the melancholy hoots of innumerable fog-horns.

"It's like a herd of cows coming down Fair Hill and along the quays to the boats!" exclaimed Sally.

"Cork must be a grand city to live in!" said the boy thoughtfully. "I've forgotten though Kitty has told me heaps about it. Now you can tell me more."

They went slowly across the deck. The ship was slowing down. Gradually it became still, swaying a little but not moving forward.

All around them ghostly ships rose up into

the grey mist. There were masts and funnels and vague shapes looming darkly. A man stared down at them from a nearby steamer. He was smoking a cigarette and the tiny red glow looked warm and friendly.

"Wish I was old enough to smoke," murmured Dom. "Hi! There's the steward!"

A thin, mournful-looking man in a very crumpled uniform came shuffling in tattered slippers across the deck. He nodded at the brother and sister.

"Ye poor childer!" he sighed. "First time at sea and this is what they let ye in for!"

"Tisn't *my* first time, Mr Mangan," Dominick objected. "I've been over from Cork to London and back again. It's Sally's first time!"

"No it isn't!" protested Sally. "I've been down to Cobh and back again. It was lovely!"

"Two sea-bitten mariners!" cried the man admiringly. "Isn't it grand how the young get about nowadays. Before ye're my age I expect ye'll have been to the North Pole or mebbe the moon. Tis a wonderful age we're living in. No doubt about that!"

"I would like to go to the South Pole!" confessed Sally.

The steward propped himself against the rail.

"Might I ask what ye'd be going there for?" he demanded. "What's wrong wid the North Pole? Isn't it good enough for ye?"

"I thought it might be warmer at the South Pole," she answered. "It does sound dreadful cold at the North Pole."

The steward rubbed his nose with the back of his hand.

"I was never one for schoolin or eddication," he muttered. "But it's my belief that when it comes to ice and snow and coldness, the South Pole isn't a haporth better than the North."

"I wonder why you never hear people talking about the South Pole," said Sally. "It's always the North Pole."

Dominick had never thought about the South Pole or the North Pole either. He said nothing, only stared into the fog.

"I wouldn't know," he told Sally. "This I will say! Ye're the first I've heard worriting about the South Pole or the North Pole. What I say is this. Let them keep out of my way and I'll keep out of theirs. What's worriting me is—shall I tell you what is worriting me?"

"What?" asked Sally and Dominick together.

"Food!" said the steward in a dismal tone. "I'm the chap that's responsible for the meals and we're running short. Tis lucky we haven't a full complement this journey, very lucky indeed."

"Why?" asked Dominick.

The steward folded his arms across his chest.

"I'll tell ye for why. We're running short of bacon, eggs, beef, bread and everything else. We were late on our schedule, so we didn't take on all the cabin stores we should have taken at Cork. We meant to send a boat ashore to collect supplies. But here we are too far from shore and we'll have to wait till morning and hope the fog will clear by then."

Sally felt thankful for the big breakfast she had eaten. Dominick was already hungry again.

"I can smell the dinner," he said, sniffing.

The steward nodded.

"Ye can! So can I! But there's tonight and tomorrow and the day after. If the fog doesn't lift soon, what will we do then?"

He glanced sharply from Dominick to Sally. They didn't know.

"Have ye never heard what shipwrecked mariners do when their stores run short and they've nothing to eat?"

Sally shook her head. Dominick looked horror-stricken.

The steward smiled grimly.

"I can see ye've read yer books, young lad. Tell yer sister!"

Dominick glared at the man.

"Tell her yourself, Mr Mangan. I won't."

Steward Mangan stood up straight.

"They eat one another!" he told Sally. "That's right, isn't it?' he added, turning to the boy.

Dominick nodded, looking very serious.

Sally gasped.

"They couldn't!" she cried indignantly. "It would be horrid. It would be wicked."

She hoped they were only joking. Yet the man and the boy stared at one another with gloomy faces.

"Don't fret!" said Mr Mangan kindly. "It mayn't come to that and we've a good dinner before us. Eat slowly and twill last longer. Besides, ye're only a skinny little creature. Yer brother has a bit more flesh on his bones. I'll be off now. I've to polish the knives and forks. We'll eat our last meal dacent, so we will!"

At any other time Sally would have thought herself the luckiest girl in the world. It was true she had been forced to part with her friends and leave the only home she could remember.

But she had a sister and brother. She was journeying on a ship in a fog and she was on her way to the biggest city in the world, or maybe it was only one of the biggest.

This morning that had been happiness enough for anyone. Now she was so filled with fear, none of the good things mattered. She lived in a world where people ate one another and she was quite sure she would never be happy again, even if she was one of the lucky ones and escaped such a terrible fate.

Kitty, coming on deck, noticed her little sister's serious face and was anxious. She went seeking for Mrs Regan and found her in the galley cutting a huge loaf into slices and singing to herself.

"What ails ye, pet?" asked the woman. "Sure, ye're not feeling quare, are ye? There's not a ripple on the water and, if ye keep below where ye can't swally the fog, there's nothing to harm ye!"

Kitty shook her head.

"I'm not feeling queer. It's Sally! She's looking so white and unhappy, I'm worried about her."

Mrs Regan stopped cutting.

"The child can't be say-sick. If she was feeling that way I'd give her a sup of fizz drink. That would settle her. Tis more likely she's homesick for Cork and the friends there that were good to her. Tis all to the child's credit. But we can't have her fretting. Bring her down here!"

Up on deck Kitty found the steward and two other men climbing down to a small row-boat. Sally and Dominick were watching them.

"Would the young ones like a trip?" asked Mr Mangan. "There's just room and we'll have them back in time for dinner. We've decided, come what may," he added grimly, "we'll do our utmost to bring back a few loaves of bread to keep us from starvation—or worse!"

Dominick ran forward eagerly. Sally hung back and shook her head.

The boy turned to her. He was disappointed. She had seemed so jolly, as good or better than a brother. Now she didn't want to take the chance of going on a boat through the fog. He couldn't understand her.

"Sally will go next time," said Kitty. "She's coming with me to help Mrs Regan down below."

The boy clambered over the side. The two sisters turned away from the fog and went down to the bright warm galley.

"Is the head aching, acushla?" asked Mrs Regan, as Sally sat beside her sister on a padded seat against the bulkhead.

Sally shook her head and tried to smile.

"Is it lonesome ye are?" asked the woman

gently.

"Sure, if ye're losing yer friends, ye've found yer sister and brother and that should make up."

She leaned on the table looking down sympathetically at Sally's mournful little face.

"It isn't that," murmured Sally. "But I can't bear to think of people eating one another."

She burst into tears and laid her head on the table.

Mrs Regan gazed in amazement at Kitty.

"Sure, the poor child must be feeling very quare!" she exclaimed. "That's a terrible notion to be having in her little head."

Kitty frowned.

"Who has been telling her such nonsense?" she asked indignantly. "Don't cry, Sally! There's the girl! You've nothing to cry for. We're all friends here!"

Suddenly the stewardess beat her hands together and burst out laughing.

"I have it!" she cried. "I have it! Tis that make-game, Joe Mangan. Tis he's been giving out his wild stories to the child, God help her! Now wouldn't ye think a man of his age and experience would have more sense?"

"What did he tell you, Sally?" asked Kitty.

"He said if the fog lasted and we couldn't get

any food, we'd have to eat one another. He said I was a skinny little creature, so I'd be safe until the end comes. But I don't want to eat anyone. I'd sooner starve!"

"The poor child!" said Mrs Regan. "Listen to me now, Sally, asthore, Joe Mangan's a terrible one for yarns. He can tell a ghost story that would raise the hair on yer head and make the bravest afeard to go on deck by himself. While he's yarning, ye'd swear he believes every word he's after saying.

"Half an hour after, he's forgotten it all. Don't mind him, pet! Wait till he gets back, I'll give him the rough side of me tongue. I'll larn him to go scarifying innocent childer!"

"Did Dom believe Mr Mangan?" asked Kitty.

"He did!" answered Sally. "He's read all about it in the books."

Sally was ashamed.

"I wish I'd gone too," she said. "I'm not brave! And now I've missed my chance of rowing through the fog."

"Whisha! Don't let that bother ye!" Mrs Regan comforted her. "Ye'll have many other chances. Sure, ye're young yet. There's all kinds of adventures before ye. Make up yer mind to be a bit braver every time, then ye'll manage.

"Now would the two of ye lend a hand. That

lazy Joe Mangan's always forgetting he's a steward and running off helping other people or hindering them most likely. I'll have a word with that boyo!"

She gave Kitty a clean tablecloth for the saloon table and handed Sally a knife box filled with cutlery.

"Lay the table," she told them, "and we'll do without the bould Mangan. Serve him right if we have every bit eaten before he comes back. Hurry now! I hear the Captain raging round and there'll be blue murder if he's kept waiting!

Kitty smoothed out the cloth so that there wasn't the least crease in it. She showed Sally how to arrange the knives, forks and spoons. Then there were tumblers and wine glasses.

Mrs Regan put two bread-boards in the centre with white bread and brown cut in slices. A basket of rolls was put at the end where the Captain sat.

"Tis a good thing the stew is thick and the soup real tasty today," said Mrs Regan. "Then there's a boiled golden syrup pudding. That always puts him in a good temper. But he can't stand fog. I never knew a say captain who could. I don't like it meself, only I can stay below, thanks be!"

While his two sisters were busy preparing

the saloon table for lunch, Dominick sat huddled in the bow of the boat watching the *Wave of Tory* disappear in the fog.

He wished he had put on his coat and muffler. The fog was damp and cold. His feet were in a puddle of dirty water which slopped up and down as the men thrust their oars into the water and the boat shot forward.

The boy wished he had a chance to row. Then he would have been warmer. But he had never used an oar before and he knew this was no time to ask one of the men to teach him.

There were ships all around and he admired the way in which the small boat slipped in and out among them. If only he hadn't been so cold Dominick would have been thrilled at the sight of men peering down from the towering, cliff-like sides, with the rigging like spiders' webs, the hoarse shouts and halloings, and the monotonous hoot of the melancholy fog-horns.

He admired the machine-like rise and fall of the oars keeping perfect time, and the way in which his companions rowed without pausing as they answered hails and questions flung down at them from the upper decks.

He shivered and hugged himself to keep out the cold. The steward frowned, whistled and nodded to Dominick.

"Now is the time for ye to learn to handle an oar!" he said. "You never know when it might come in handy. Sit in here and do exactly as I tell ye!"

With one hand holding the oar he drew the boy on to the seat between his legs.

"Put yer hands above mine. When I bend forward, bend with me. When I thrust, let ye thrust. When I pull, pull yer hardest! Now! One—two, one—two! That's the lad!"

Dominick breathed hard. Joe Mangan's body shielded him from the wind. He no longer saw where they were going. He could think of nothing but gripping the oar, bending forward, stretching backward. One, two! One, two!

"Now I'll leave ye to row on yer own," said the steward, loosening his hands and leaning back.

"One, two! " he counted. "One, two! Don't get flustrificated. Go steady. Good! Good! Hallo! What's wrong?"

Dominick was warmer now. He was wishing the other rowers would work a little quicker, so that he could show how strong he was, when the oar was gripped underneath the water and he almost let go.

"What's wrong?" repeated the steward. Then he chuckled.

"Ye've caught a crab! Pull it in, boy, and we'll

have it wid our tay!"

Dominick glanced down. He could see no sign of a crab. He looked at the steward suspiciously. A sailor pulled on the oar. It came loose and there they were, rowing easily and steadily.

"They call that catching a crab," explained the sailor. "You'll do it many times before you're used to rowing. It means you dipped the oar too deeply, that's all. When that happens, pull it out and start fresh. You'll soon be used to it."

"I'm going to learn on the lake in Victoria Park when I'm in London," Dominick told him proudly.

"Good lad! Learn all you can while you have the chance. You can never know too much. Now sit back while I take the oar. It's a bit tricky here."

Dominick slipped over to his old seat. Sitting still, he felt colder than before.

"Wish I could have kept on," he thought. "Won't the boys stare when they see how I've learned to row."

At last they came to clusters of small boats, steam launches, a tug drawing a string of barges piled with planks, another with a huge vessel packed with barrels. The steward and the other men rested on their oars.

"Hi there!" called Joe Mangan, looking up at

a small dark man staring down at them from the deck of a tramp steamer almost hidden under a mountain of dirty fleeces. "Is the River Stores anywhere abouts?"

"You've arrived!" bawled the dark man, pointing up the river. "Land at the next steps and you'll see it staring you in the face!"

"Hallo sonny!" he called to Dominick. "Looking for a berth?"

Dominick was bewildered. He shook his head.

"Why don't you take the child back and give him a cup of hot cocoa and a blanket?" demanded the dark man. "That's no way to treat a poor orphan!"

Joe Mangan looked worried. The other men laughed.

"I should have told him to bring a coat," muttered the steward. "Those bits of pullovers have no warmth in them."

"Will I throw down a sheepskin?" asked the small dark man.

All, except Dominick, laughed at this.

"Wish they would," thought the boy. "I'm perished with the cold. Sally doesn't know how lucky she is to be on the nice warm steamer."

They pulled in at a double flight of muddy, slippery steps. Joe Mangan tied the boat securely to a post set firmly in the bank.

"Come along, lad!" he said to Dominick. "A bit of a trot will stir the blood in yer veins and mebbe we'll find a sup of hot tay."

"Ye're a lucky young fella to be seeing the world," he told Dominick. "Why wouldn't the little sister come? Feared of boats, or the fog, or just lazy?"

The boy shook his head as he marched between the steward and the two other men.

"I don't rightly know. I think she was just miserable about people eating one another if they're starving."

Joe Mangan laughed.

"Didn't worry ye, lad, did it?" he asked. "Ye know a joke when ye hear one, don't yer? Ye're smart!"

Dominick flushed.

"Isn't it true?" he asked. "I had read about it in a sea story. Some sailors were shipwrecked and starving. They drew lots. I didn't really believe it till you said it might happen on the *Wave of Tory*."

He looked up at the grinning steward.

"So it wasn't true!" he said. "You were just teasing. But Sally believed you. So did I."

"Aren't you the eejit, Joe Mangan," said the mate who had been listening quietly. "What call have you to be frightening children? You should know better."

Joe Mangan stopped grinning.

"I'm sorry I frightened the little sister," he said. "I never thought she'd take it serious. Sure, ye can tell her twas only a bit of gas. I'll have to tell her a funny story to make up. And while we're at the Stores, we may find a clean sack to wrap yer shoulders in. Look, there's the place!"

Dominick saw a big white board at the side of the road. On it he read in black letters:

RIVER STORES.

Provisions for Ships, River Steamers, Picnic Parties.

No Credit. Terms, Strictly Cash.

5
Dinner on Board

he Stores was a ramshackle wooden building with a corrugated iron roof. A counter went round three sides; a counter made of orange boxes with gaps here and there to enable the men selling to pass in and out. Sacks and boxes were piled at the back on the counters and the floor.

The noise of men shouting for what they wanted and men calling back the price made Dominick so bewildered he backed into a corner behind Joe Mangan and peered out at the crowd.

The shop was full when they entered. Every moment it became more and more crowded. So many ships were held up by the fog that provisions had become scarce.

Men trudged up from the shore carrying bags

and baskets and this made others realize that they were hungry, that they had no food in reserve and would be hungrier before nightfall.

Dominick had never seen so many strange-looking men in his life before. There were pale men with thin fair hair wearing faded blue coats and trousers, black men with frizzy mops, flat noses, thick lips and large dark eyes, smiling, frowning, restless, bigger than most of their companions, yet allowing themselves to be pushed this way and that by men half their size.

Growing tired of standing near the door while others came in behind them and made a rapid way to the counter, these dark seamen gave a thrust, and there they were at the counter, still silent, still smiling.

Slight coffee-coloured men talked eagerly with one another but fell into silence when spoken to by strangers. There were men so brown they seemed made of bronze, only their eyes and teeth keeping their original colour. They lounged up from tiny yachts and made their way forward from the outskirts of the crowd.

Dominick was squeezed tight into his corner. He tugged at Joe Mangan's coat. The tall thin man looked down at him over his shoulder.

"Hallo, lad! Getting warm? Don't vex yourself. When we've bought all we came for, I'll charge a way out. Hold on to me and ye won't go wrong. I'll see ye righted! Not scared, are ye?"

"Of course not!" replied Dominick.

Yet he was. He couldn't see between the bodies which closed him in, and the rough corners of the boxes he was pressed against seemed to be cutting him into ribbons.

A fat man with a smooth face, shining with sweat, was serving at the other side of the counter. He paused to wipe his forehead with a tattered red handkerchief and saw Dominick.

"Are the boys flattening ye out?" he asked. "Come across here and get a breath of air."

He leaned forward, put his hands under Dominick's arms and pulled him over.

"Like drawing a winkle from its shell!" he chuckled, setting the boy down beside him.

"Now you can make yourself useful!" the fat man told Dominick. "Stand guard over there between the bread and the flour. When I call out, get snappy!"

Dominick frowned. He had been longing to escape from his uncomfortable corner. But to be lifted about like a baby and ordered, not asked, to help, annoyed him.

Yet he soon found himself handing over the

different goods—four large loaves, six small, one bag of flour, a bag of salt, a bar of soap. He made mistakes, giving a small loaf instead of a large; soap instead of salt.

The fat man winked at his mistakes, nodded when he was correct and, when the crowd of seafaring men began to dwindle, beckoned him closer.

"What's yer age, Dom?"

"I'm ten and a half!" answered the boy proudly.

The fat man sighed.

"Ten and a half! A great lump of a lad like yerself and only ten and a half. I thought you'd be fourteen at the least. I was going to offer you a job, a good steady job."

"Here?" asked Dominick.

"Here! Messenger boy to the River Stores, ten shillings a week and all found. Well, come back in another three years and a half and the job's yours."

"I'd want more money then," said Dominick firmly.

"What's this? More money? Why?"

"Because I'll be three and a half years older!"

The store-keeper laughed.

"Pon me word! You're a smart lad, even if you are only ten and a half. Well, come back when you're fourteen and we'll see what we can do."

"Will you be here when I'm fourteen?" asked Dominick.

The man became serious.

"If you're like this at ten and a half, when you're fourteen you won't be looking for a messenger boy's job. You'll want to be a partner or run a stores of your own."

"Finished the deal, Dom?" asked Joe Mangan.

He had been listening. So had the two men with him.

"Come along!" said Joe. "Ye'll need yer dinner after this."

He turned to the other men.

"Ten and a half," he said, "and he's turned down a good offer and fixed his future!"

"Put this sack over your head," said the fat man, picking up a clean sack and ripping it down one side. "That will keep out rain and wind. Don't forget! If you're passing in three and a half years' time, look in."

"Goodbye, and thank you very much!" said Dominick.

He pulled the sack over his head and went towards the door. He stood aside to let the three men go first but Joe Mangan gave him a push.

"Ye lead the way, lad! We know we're safe

with a smart young man like ye leading us."

They all laughed. It was a friendly laugh, so Dominick didn't mind, though he couldn't see anything funny in what the steward had said.

Joe Mangan carried a sack of flour on his back. The other men loaded a wheelbarrow with potatoes, cabbages and a leg of mutton. Next they piled on a whole cheese like a cartwheel and a sack of loaves.

"Not much risk for the fat ones on board the *Wave of Tory*," chuckled Joe Mangan, winking at Dominick.

The boy flushed.

"I did read it," he said. "I suppose it happened a long, long time ago.

Joe swung him into the boat and scrambled after. The men handed in the provisions. Joe stowed them in the bow and under the seats.

The sack fell off Dominick's shoulders but he was so hot from the work he didn't notice it. When they cast away and were once more going out over the river with the fog closing in all round them, he began to shiver and was thankful when the mate picked up the sack and put it round his shoulders again.

"You're a great little lad," he said. "Only you must learn to take a bit of care. Your sister wouldn't thank us if we took you back sneezing and coughing. And Mrs Regan would murder us! She hates colds going the round."

It took longer to row the full boat back to the steamer than when they had been finding their way to the shore. Yet not one of the four in that leaky, creaking little row-boat bothered.

The men turned up their collars and took shifts at rowing. Dominick snuggled inside the dry, warm sack. He felt he was an adventurer. Though he was only ten and a half, already he had the offer of a job.

All the boys he knew, who were older than himself, talked about the jobs they wanted. Now he felt just as old as they were and terribly proud. Wait till he told Kitty and Sally! They'd be proud of their brother.

"Ahoy there!" called Joe Mangan. "*Wave of Tory*, ahoy!"

The ship hadn't seemed very large when they were leaving it. Now it towered above them, massive and imposing.

"Like a castle!" thought Dominick.

A man looked over the side and there they were at the foot of a wooden ladder.

"Up you go, lad!" said the mate. "Hold tight now, for the wood is desprit slippy!"

Dominick stood up on the seat and, reaching out, made a grab at the ladder. His fingers slipped on the greasy surface and he stumbled forward.

The sack fell into the water and he would have gone with it only Joe Mangan caught his arm and dragged him up.

"Ye're a regular boyo!" he declared. "Go steady and mind where ye set yer feet. That water wouldn't make too good a drink, I'm thinking!"

Dominick went very carefully. It seemed a long way up to the deck, for he was tired out.

"Aren't ye very unlucky, Joe Mangan," said one of the men coiling ropes on the deck. "If ye'd only been here ten minutes ago ye'd have had the chance of a bit and sup. Now there's nothing to do but wash the dishes. Mebbe the young lad will give ye a hand!"

Never had Dominick felt so hungry.

"If there's no dinner for him, there won't be for me," he told himself. "Only I would have thought Kitty would save me a bit!"

He went slowly down to the saloon. Kitty and Sally were there with Mrs Regan, eating hot, golden syrup pudding and drinking steaming cups of tea.

Dominick stood in the doorway looking at them.

"Whisha! The child's come at last! Sit down

now while I fetch yer dinner. It's keeping hot on the range," cried Mrs Regan, jumping up at once.

"Won't there be any for Mr Mangan?" asked Dominick. "The man who let down the ladder said there wouldn't be any left. Couldn't he have some of mine?"

Mrs Regan put her hands on her hips and shook with laughter.

"Now if that's not a joke. Let him take a bite off the playboy that gave him the message. Him and his tales about dacent people aiting one another."

They all laughed. Dominick sat beside Sally and began to tell about the River Stores and the strange people he had seen there.

Mrs Regan arrived with a plate of stew. Kitty poured him a glass of lemonade and he stopped talking to eat. He was glad he hadn't to share with the steward, though the plate was big and piled with pieces of salt fish, potatoes, onions, squares of yellow turnip, slices of carrot and butter beans.

Dominick ate every scrap of it, two rolls and a lump of cheese. Then he settled down to golden syrup pudding and a cup of tea.

He told about the fine job he'd been offered.

"Ye won't need a job in an old riverside

stores," declared Mrs Regan. "Ye'll be an officer in an Atlantic liner or something in the civil service when ye grow up. Ye'll be on one of those ships where they have dinner at the right time and don't call lunch dinner," she added scornfully. "I can see ye're a lad wid brains and character."

Dominick stretched his legs under the table and filled his mouth with hot pudding.

"This is a lovely voyage!" he said.

6
Friends from Home

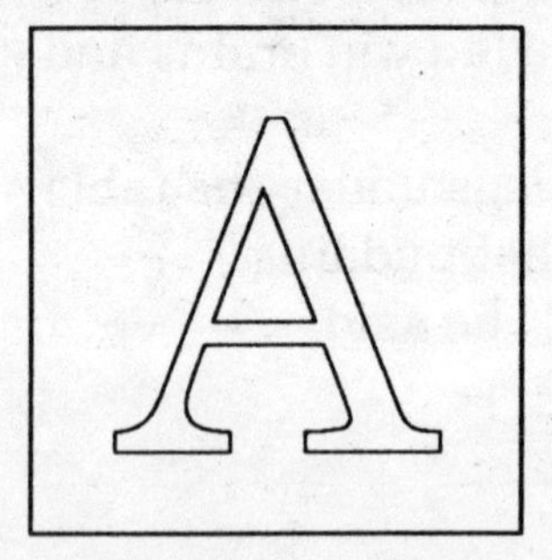

fter dinner Mrs Regan sat darning and sewing on buttons. She had a grand basket fitted with reels of cotton and silk, an ivory crochet hook, coloured knitting-needles, skeins of wool and silk and, what Sally thought the height of luxury, a silver thimble.

Kitty was reading while Dominick taught Sally to play draughts. He won three games then sat back and stared at her.

"You're not trying to play," he declared. "Don't you like it?"

Sally shook her head.

"I like chess better," she said quietly, hoping she didn't sound conceited. "We used to play draughts at the Mooneys until Mr Mooney joined a chess club. Then he taught Janey and me so that he'd have plenty of practice. He was one of the best players in the Cork Club."

Kitty looked up from her book.

"I'd love to play chess. It looks so elegant. Could you teach us?"

Sally felt frightened and wished she hadn't spoken.

"Serves me right for bragging," she thought.

"I could teach you the moves," she answered. "I'm not very good at it. Janey Mooney could always beat me. She could beat her father. She was the only one who could."

"Have you a set of chess-men?" asked Kitty in amazement. "And a board?"

"No!" Sally told her sister, feeling happy again.

"That's aisy fixed!" cried Mrs Regan, slapping her darning down on the table. "I'll borry the Captain's. He's always raging because he never has a soul to play wid!"

Sally was terrified.

Suppose the Captain wanted her to play with him. It would be much worse than playing with Mr Mooney.

Luckily Captain MacCarthy was on deck. He grudged the short time he had spent below eating his dinner. He had a cup of hot, strong coffee sent up to him every half-hour, for he dreaded the treachery of fog, far more than the worst storm, and disliked going below until the weather was clear.

Sally was ashamed of herself. Yet when Mrs Regan explained why they could borrow the Captain's chess-men she felt happy and confident again.

Mrs Regan returned with a brown wooden box which had the Captain's initials "P. MacC" carved on it. They all leaned forward to watch her tipping out the pieces on the large heavy board. Then they looked at Sally inquiringly. She was timid yet terribly proud.

Half the chess-men were red, the other half white. Kitty picked up a knight and stared at it curiously.

"Are you sure the Captain won't mind us using his pieces?" she asked. "They must be very precious. They're made of ivory."

Sally thought of Mr Mooney's set, bought one Saturday on the Coal Quay. They were chipped and grubby. Yet he would not allow Janey or Sally to touch them unless he was there. Here was the Captain letting strangers handle his precious ivory pieces in his absence.

"He must think an awful lot of Mrs Regan," she thought.

She opened the folded board and put out the pieces. Her fingers were trembling and the red king rolled from the table.

Dominick caught this as it fell and they settled down to the best game in the world.

Although Mrs Regan had watched the Captain playing many a time, she did not know the moves and looked at Sally with great respect.

Sally soon forgot her fears. She explained the moves and when at last Kitty and Dominick ventured to play a game while she watched and guided them, Sally felt the Mooneys would have been proud of her.

"Wish Janey was here!" she thought regretfully.

The chess-board was put on one side while they had tea. Captain MacCarthy came down and drank a cup standing while Kitty thanked him for lending his chess-men.

He stared at Sally as her sister explained that she was teaching them.

"Aren't you proud of your little sister?" he asked Dominick.

"She's another big sister," the boy explained. "I'm the youngest!"

The Captain laughed, rolled up a thin slice of buttered toast and crammed it into his mouth, giving Sally's hair a tug as he went out.

"Thanks be, you're the only passengers!" he

said. "If this fog clears, we'll play a game together yet. I wish my young ones at home had your brains."

Mrs Regan came in just in time to hear this. She looked at Sally with dancing eyes.

"There's praise for ye! Only don't be too consated over it. If ye could speak twelve languages or sing and dance to beat the band, he'd think nothing of it. But play chess and he's yer friend for life!"

The mate came down for his tea and put on the wireless. So, to Sally's relief, the chess-men and the board were taken back to the Captain's cabin.

"Now we've learned the moves we'll play on wet Sunday evenings," said Kitty. "Anyway you need a rest. You can't be teaching us all the time."

That night when they went to their berths Sally felt she had been on the *Wave of Tory* for years. She tried to wonder what the Mooneys were doing and where they were. They had become like people in a book or in a dream—strange and unreal. Only Janey remained as she always had been.

Sally's eyes were closing when the ship began to move slowly. She tried to look out through the little round window but the fog still pressed against it.

From all sides sounded fog-horns and signals. Lying in her berth she pitied the Captain out there in the cold and mist. How he must long for the sun to break through.

"I love the sun!" thought Sally.

Next day men from other ships came aboard visiting. Then Sally found a shelf of books which Mrs Regan said she could borrow from. She began to read *Uncle Tom's Cabin*. She read curled up on the sofa, forgetting fog, the ship she was on, even Mrs Regan.

Kitty and Dominick came in search of her.

Tears were rolling down her cheeks but she read on.

"Come away," whispered Kitty to Dominick. "I'd hate to have anyone see me crying over a book!"

When it was time for tea Sally was laughing. She kept *Uncle Tom's Cabin* in her lap and told the others the story as far as she'd read.

"I tried it once," said Mrs Regan thoughtfully. "And it nearly broke the heart in me. Sure, I never got to the funny part. I must try again."

"I never read it at all," sighed Kitty. "I never had the time for such a big book. I like them small with big print."

By bed time Sally had finished the story and

the fog was thicker than ever.

"I'll be able to read another book tomorrow," she decided and fell asleep the moment she put her head on the pillow.

Sally dreamed of Uncle Tom and thought that she too was a runaway slave. She never quite forgot that dream.

When she woke again, Kitty was brushing her hair.

"We're going up the river," she said. "By the time we've finished breakfast we'll be in London."

To Sally's surprise her sister sounded pleased and excited.

"Do you like London?" she asked in amazement, as she pulled off her nightgown.

"I do! It's so big and grand. You never know what's going to happen next. Besides, a girl has chances in London."

Sally blinked.

"Don't you want to go back to Cork?" she asked fearfully. "Don't you want to go home?"

Kitty laid down the brush and gazed thoughtfully through the porthole at the waves churned up by the speeding ship.

She didn't see them. She saw instead the old houses on Wise's Hill and, farther back in time, the pleasant house she had lived in with her father and mother when she was no older than Sally.

That was home and she'd never forget it.

She looked at Sally, splashing in the warm soapy water, and thought of her sitting on the steps, not knowing what was going to happen, lonely and frightened. How could that be home?

"One day," she said, "we may go back and make a home for ourselves. It will be something to work for. We can go over and look round in the holidays. Just now our home is wherever we can be together. Don't think of yourself as being an emigrant. You and Dom and I are adventurers. You wanted to go to the North Pole, or was it the South? Just now your Pole is London. Jump up and conquer it!"

They both laughed.

"I don't feel homesick any more!" declared Sally, tying her boot-laces. She stood up.

"Kitty! Have we really a father? Where is he? Why doesn't he write? Or, maybe, he does write to you?"

She gazed hopefully at her sister. Kitty frowned.

"Don't ask me to explain now. It's all puzzling and rather sad. We should go into breakfast. Come along!"

She put her arm round Sally's shoulder and

they went into the saloon.

Breakfast was very exciting. Joe Mangan was laying the table in the saloon when they arrived. There was coffee and grape-fruit, fried bacon and eggs, crisp brown, gorgeously smelling sausages, crescent rolls, lemon marmalade and dainty shells of butter.

Dominick was helping himself and with each fresh dish his eyes grew bigger and bigger.

"Did we bring all these yesterday?" he asked.

The steward chuckled.

"Most of it! The rest comes from the fridge. Aren't we the lucky ones to be living nowadays and not in the bad old times when we'd have been thankful to get stale water and wormy biscuits."

Dominick looked at him scornfully.

"You mean when people ate one another?" he said, with his head on one side.

"Isn't he bold?" thought Sally admiringly. "I'd never dare to speak to Mr Mangan like that!"

Joe Mangan laughed.

"I'm not sure I wouldn't sooner be chewing a nice fat little boy or girl instead of wormy biscuits. Settle down to it and eat up. There'll be no lunch and dear knows what time we'll be really in. The Pool is packed with delayed craft and we must take our turn at the docks. So eat all ye can!"

"What Pool?" asked Dominick.

"The Pool of London!" answered the steward.

"Geography at this hour of the morning!" exclaimed Mrs Regan, sweeping in, a duster in one hand, a bunch of keys in the other. "The Captain's lepping mad, poor man! Ye'd think the sky would fall if the *Wave of Tory* is ten minutes late. Just as if twas an old bus in the street!"

"Now don't forget, children, the minute ye have finished eating, go to the cabin and pack. I have to make everything ready for the next trip before I leave the ship—and I have me family waiting on me."

"I didn't know you had a family," said Kitty thoughtfully. "Isn't it very good of you to leave them and come away to look after strange people?"

Mrs Regan looked at her kindly.

"Whisha, tis ye have the good heart. Sure I love me job and I hate leaving me family. But we'd be as poor as church mice if I didn't work and I can't bear to see young ones going short. Now eat up and don't leave a crumb!"

It didn't take the young travellers long to pack, though Kitty was much more particular than Mrs Mooney had been about folding clothes neatly so that they wouldn't have the least wrinkle.

At last her smart suitcase, Dominick's knapsack and Sally's old canvas bag were packed and stood side by side. Sally wandered into the saloon and wished she could stay longer.

"Perhaps we'll be going back to Cork one day," she thought. "Maybe it will be for ever or just a holiday. I must learn to play chess really well. Then I won't be scared of Captain MacCarthy. Wouldn't it be wonderful if I could play well enough to beat him!"

Dominick put his head in at the door.

"Come on deck!" he said. "There's all the ships in the world crowded together. You don't want to stay stuck in this stuffy hole."

"I was just saying goodbye!" explained Sally.

Dominick was puzzled. There wasn't anybody in the cabin. So Sally was just saying goodbye to an empty room. Already the boy liked his young sister, though he thought her strange. Maybe all the people in Cork were that way!

He gazed at her thoughtfully. How would she get on among the smart London people? He'd have to stand up for her.

"Come along, Sally!" he said. "It's great fun up on deck."

They went up together and stood against the rail. Ships crowded in on all sides, so close they could have jumped aboard several. Men stood in groups, peering ahead. One boat was crowded with holiday makers, crumpled and weary after an unexpected night away from home.

"What a wonderful castle!" Sally cried, clutching her brother's arm.

The fog was thinner now and she saw grey towers and battlements rising above the river. Low down at the water's edge was a wide gateway, while between the castle walls and the river was a roadway where motors hustled by.

"That's the Tower—the Tower of London!" Dominick told her, proud to show his knowledge.

"Do they still bring the prisoners there in boats?" asked Sally in a low whisper.

Sally was usually top in history at school but she often forgot that times change and grieved about the troubles and tragic happenings that no longer existed.

Dominick was shocked.

"No, indeed they don't, any more than they execute people on Tower Hill now. That's the

Tower! I've been all over it. People live there and there aren't any prisoners. They used to bring them in boats to the Water Gate but that was long ago!"

"I am glad!" murmured Sally. "Oh, look! There's a bridge up in the air!"

"That's the Tower Bridge," her brother told her. "Now you'll see the road go up."

Sally's mouth as well as her eyes opened wide when she saw the bridge break in two. Each part rose in the air against the twin towers and slowly the ships passed on, hooting in triumph.

The *Wave of Tory* edged nearer and nearer to the bank. So slowly did it approach that Sally and Dominick could hardly believe it was moving at all. Yet they were leaving the main stream of traffic behind and gliding along a quay.

On each side were great lorries being loaded. They throbbed and quivered. As one moved away from the river another took its place. Men shouted and waved, crouched over their engines, hauled and lifted sacks and crates.

Dominick said something to Sally. She smiled but could not hear for the din around them.

Kitty clutched her sister's arm and pointed. Sally saw a horse-drawn cart. There were people in it waving. Kitty and Dominick waved back.

"Friends!" said Sally to herself, suddenly feeling safe. She had a brother and a sister, and here were friends coming to welcome them.

Sally had thought the misty river with the strange old Tower and the marvellous moving bridge so wonderful she felt she could look at them forever.

She hadn't wanted to leave the *Wave of Tory* where the little cabin had so soon become familiar and the crew like old acquaintances. She had feared coming to this huge strange city. Now the waving hands, the smiles of greeting rid her of this dread as if they were friendly winds blowing away mists.

"I was wondering how we'd go home," murmured Kitty.

There was too much noise for her companions to know what she was saying. Now two men slipped from the cart and made their way through the crowd, between lorries and trucks, right to the edge of the quay, and gazed upward.

One tipped his cap. The other was bare-headed.

"So ye've friends to meet ye," said Joe Mangan's voice behind them. "I've had the bags brought up and the gangway is ready. Here's Mrs Regan to say goodbye!"

The big woman came from behind him. There were tears in her eyes as she hugged each one of them.

"If I'm not heart-scalded to be parting from ye!" she lamented. "Twas the happiest voyage I've known and the easiest. Most times we have a round dozen and they saysick and discontented and quarrelsome.

"I have the address and it won't be my fault if we don't meet again. Stand by one another and one day ye'll be coming down to Rogerson's Quay on the way home. Here's Danny with the bags. Are them chaps relations coming to meet ye?"

"Friends from home!" answered Kitty.

7
Is this Home?

ally found herself being lifted from the ship, carried along a gangway which tilted upwards, for the heavily laden *Wave of Tory* lay low in the water, then swung up to a cart which smelt of cabbages and potatoes.

Behind her Joe Mangan was calling farewells to the "young ones from Cork," greetings to people with familiar names, like Peter Quinn and James Hegarty.

Sally was soon settled on a bench between a thin, severe-looking woman with a very pale face, dressed in black, and a small fidgety man who grumbled and whistled alternately.

The bags were thrown up on the cart by two men who patted Kitty and Dominick and gazed mournfully at Sally, telling her not to be frightened or homesick.

The one with the cap settled himself in front, shook the reins and waved the whip. The horse gave a heave to the left, a heave to the right and there they were, swaying along behind a lorry, the *Wave of Tory* out of sight and all London before them.

Dominick nodded reassuringly at his young sister. Kitty smiled at her. They both looked startled and Sally wondered if they were going the right way.

There was so much to see and hear, she was too bewildered to see or hear anything. She shut her eyes. Maybe when she opened them again she would be back in Cork.

No! Cork was over the sea. She might never see it again. She was as much an emigrant as Janey Mooney.

Through the din of crashing lorries and screeching motors, the small fidgety man shouted names in Sally's ear. The woman on the other side pursed her lips, then smiled at Sally.

She was too bewildered even to wonder who they were. The cart went on over small bridges, waited at waterways until other bridges swung into place and the traffic surged across.

Kitty and Dominick were listening to an old man who leaned forward with both hands on a crooked stick. His small bright eyes darted this way and that; his tongue, darting like a pink serpent, repeatedly licked his lips.

Next to Kitty sat a tall stout handsome woman with black hair shining like satin. She smiled and nodded but never said a word.

"I like her!" thought Sally. "She's sensible. She knows it's no use talking. I'm glad we have friends. You can't really be lonesome if you have friends!"

The cart came to a jerky stop in a paved triangular space with high dilapidated houses on all sides. They hadn't the faded grandeur of the houses in Wise's Hill.

Instead of steep steps going up there were shallow steps going down to basements with bare windows.

Sally had never seen so many rusty iron bars in her life, for the basement windows had bars across and the gates were padlocked.

At every upper window women with tousled hair leaned on the sills and gazed with blank unwelcoming eyes at the cart and its occupants.

"Down you come, girleen!" said a young man, so big Sally thought him a giant.

He seized her by the elbows and lifted her to the ground.

"Welcome to the Triangle!" he said. "I'm

Roger O'Keefe, at your service. I'll be seeing you tonight. There's a ceilidhe at the Club!"

"I'll be there!" said the stout woman.

Kitty and Dominick sprang to the ground beside Sally. The three pieces of luggage were handed down.

The cart backed at once. They heard faint goodbyes and "God bless yous!" Then they stood on the deserted pavement.

Tousled women still looked from the windows, only now they were smiling.

"Another of them Irish emigrants!" said one. "Only, by the looks of her, she could be worse!"

Kitty laughed.

"We'd be strangers in the Triangle if we were living here for a hundred years!"

Kitty pushed open a door, and they crowded into a small, dingy hall. A narrow staircase made its way up into darkness.

The walls of the basement were white-washed, the big barred window shone and all around were giant nasturtiums, trained to climb the walls. Bees had discovered them and a pleasant hum rose into the foggy air.

"Hold the banisters!" warned Kitty. "The corners are tricky."

Up, up they went, past closed doors and partly opened ones. Radios squeaked and chattered, there were whispers, there were shouts. The stairs grew more and more narrow, changing at last to a small, winding staircase.

An old woman stuck out her head and sighed.

"Another one for the Triangle," she muttered. "They come and they never go."

They reached the top and Kitty put a tiny key into the lock of the door which barred their way.

"This is our very own!" she said, over her shoulder.

They put down their luggage. Sally looked round and started back in amazement. Before her, at the other side of the room, a wide window reached from side to side.

Right opposite, through a gap between the two tallest houses in the Triangle, rose the mast of a ship. A monkey sat perched there and, when Sally pointed, it danced up and down, chattered, pointed back and scratched its chest.

The longer she looked, the more she saw.

Factory chimneys mingled with masts and funnels and when she went over to the window she discovered, straight below, a new bridge across which went an unending procession of strange-looking men and women.

She saw sailors who rolled from side to side as they walked, men carrying sacks so heavy the carriers were bowed nearly to the ground.

There were yellow men with narrow, slit eyes and one wore a fawn-coloured robe with a string of big, brown, carved beads hanging from his belt. He let them slip through his fingers as if he were saying the Rosary.

There were men whose faces were golden brown and others so dark they might have been made of chocolate. Some were black and the teeth in their laughing mouths looked like the whitest ivory. Sally, who had been reading *Uncle Tom's Cabin* on the boat, wondered anxiously if these were escaped slaves.

Two young women in silk robes with long scarves draped over their dark hair passed over the bridge as if they were floating on air.

Kitty came across the room and put her hand on her young sister's shoulder.

"Isn't it wonderful!" she said. "Like moving pictures or illustrations to a story-book. When you know London you'll understand how lucky we are to live here."

"How did it all happen?" asked Sally.

"Help me lay the table and I'll tell you. Dom has gone out to buy fish and chips. We'll have tea and bread and jam as well. Look! The cups and saucers are in the cupboard over there. When we've had a rest we'll fix up where you're to sleep.

"Isn't it lucky my holidays aren't over till Monday so we've heaps of time. It was a big rush to get to Cork. We had a chance of a cheap passage, so we took it!"

The table was square. Kitty pulled it out of the corner and placed it in front of the window so that, while Sally ate, she could look out on this strange world she had come to.

There was a red checked tablecloth. The teacups, saucers and plates looked like blue Wedgwood ware. They weren't. But Sally thought them beautiful. The teapot was like the brown one her friends had used on Wise's Hill and, when Kitty put a loaf on the wooden platter, her younger sister began to feel this was really home.

Suddenly the door burst open and Dominick, clutching a steaming, untidy, paper parcel, burst into the room.

"I was served first!" he announced. "You should have seen the crowd waiting when I squeezed up to the counter."

"That's cheating!" Kitty said severely. "You must take your turn."

"I didn't push hard!" Dominick told her. "Besides, I'm always in a hurry. The others aren't! Is the oven hot?"

Sally watched while Kitty brought a dish out

from the gas oven and tipped out three golden brown pieces of fish and a shower of crisp chipped potatoes. These were put in the oven while Kitty made a pot of tea and Dominick cut thin slices of bread and butter.

When they sat down at the table by the window Sally discovered she was hungry. She ate steadily while the others talked away of places she had never heard about and people she didn't know existed.

Kitty put her elbows on the table and smiled.

"When you're ready we want to hear about Cork," she said. "You'll meet other people from Ireland and they'll all want to hear your story but we have the first claim. Tell us what it really is like over there. We all hope to go back and some lucky ones spend their holidays there."

She sighed and looked beyond the masts and chimneys rising into the misty air.

"Perhaps when I'm as old as the hills I really will go back!"

Sally leaned easily in her chair and began to examine her future home. The room was big with a bookcase beside the door, so like the one Mr Mooney had sold only last week that Sally thought Kitty must have bought it. But how could that be?

"That's exactly like the bookcase at the

Mooneys'," she said. "Mr Mooney sold it to a man on the Coal Quay in Cork."

"What did he do with the books?" Kitty wanted to know.

"He gave them to his friends. He had them all packed up ready to go on the ship but he found he had too much luggage. Poor Mr Mooney! He nearly cried at parting with them."

"Why didn't he sell his books?" asked Dominick curiously.

Sally shook her head.

"Oh no! He wouldn't do that! He'd had most of them all his life. So he felt he couldn't sell them. He gave them away to people who would care for them. I wish he'd given one to me!"

"You can read all my books!" Kitty told her. "Besides, you can join the public library. Dom belongs! Now we must wash up."

"I'll do it," Sally offered. "I always did the washing-up at Mooneys' and the shopping as well as the cleaning."

Kitty laughed.

"Thank goodness! I hate buying food. Dom does that. He's wonderful. I hate washing up, and cleaning too. You'll be a godsend! But just for today you're a visitor. You must get used to the place and the people.

"Look! Through that little door! There is your

corner. It's only a box of a place but there's a window. You'll have it all to yourself! Dom's is over that side, exactly like yours. Mine is the room next this!"

Sally pushed open a narrow door and found herself in a room so small it was more like a cupboard. A folding chair stood against the wall. The window was round, like the porthole on the *Wave of Tory*. And she thought how grand it was.

"A room all to myself!" she thought. "I never had that with the Mooneys!"

Sally stood with her face pressed close to the round window, unconscious of the scene below, seeing the only home she remembered—the gaunt old house on Wise's Hill, its many friendly inhabitants and the neighbours.

They were so far away and the Mooneys would, by this time, be farther still. Maybe she would never see them again.

Tears came into her eyes and streamed down her cheeks. Then she heard someone calling her name.

"Well, Sally! How do you like it? Oh, you poor child! Don't cry, Sally! I know it's all strange, but you're with your own sister and brother. This is home!"

And there was Kitty hugging and kissing

her.

"How foolish I am!" sighed the older girl. "I'm so thankful to have you with us at last that I forget you hardly know us. Don't feel lonely, Sally! We're real fond of you and I'll do my very best to make you happy."

"What's wrong?" asked Dominick's voice. "Why is Sally crying? Has she hurt herself?"

"Sally's lonely and homesick!" explained Kitty. "I should never have left her so long. Only I thought it was great to have one of us in Cork. Don't cry, Sally! You'll never be alone again! Will she, Dom?"

"No such luck!" answered the boy with a grin.

They all laughed, and when Kitty showed Sally how the folding chair could be made into a bed with sheets, a pillow, a blanket and a plaid shawl, she no longer felt lonesome but was quite ready to go out with Dominick to buy what they needed for the week-end and to meet the neighbours.

They were half-way down the winding stairs when Kitty put her head out of the door and called after them.

"Sally, you've not told us one word about Cork! Be ready to tell us everything when you come back!"

"She'll never have the chance," Dominick

called up.

"She'll have to fight to get a word in edgeways!"

8
Marketing with Dominick

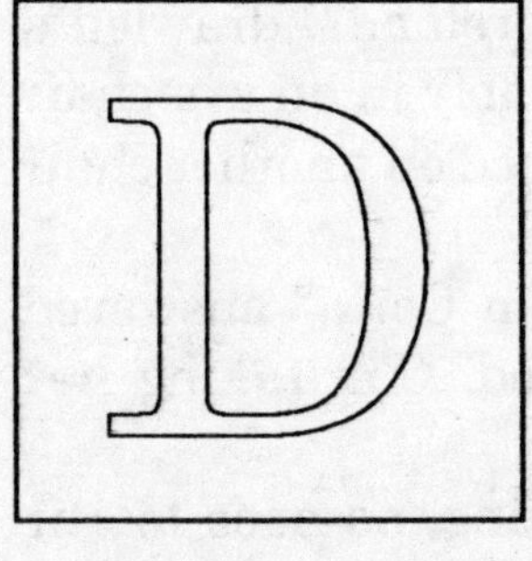

ominick had a striped canvas bag; Sally carried a basket Kitty had given her.

"What are we going to buy?" asked Sally. "Have you ever been marketing before?"

"I always do the shopping!" declared Dominick proudly. "You couldn't expect Kitty to do it. She has her job and keeps the place clean. That's enough for any girl. Besides, she's no good at managing money. She'd always give them what she's asked and you've got to bargain. You'll learn! Watch me and keep your mouth shut!"

He raced down the steps. As he passed, door after door fell open. Sally could see beyond the curious, questing eyes and faces to the rooms behind. Not one of them could compare with the neat bright rooms at the top.

Torn lace curtains, dirty windows, broken furniture, tables cluttered with unwashed dishes and the remains of the last meal met her gaze. Yet the faces were friendly, amused, and she smiled back.

"Is this the latest from Ireland?" drawled a fat man, stretched comfortably in an armchair by a window, his feet propped on another chair without a back.

"It's me sister Sally from Cork," answered Dominick, slackening speed. "I'm taking her out to see the sights."

"If it's sights she's wanting, no need to stir from the Triangle!" declared the fat man. "But you Irish are always on the run!"

He chuckled at his own wit and the children went on, down the stairs.

An old woman, so bent she had to turn her head sideways to peer at them, was sitting in her doorway.

She held out her hands to Sally.

"I seen ye on the way up," she said. "But I didn't want to bother ye till ye were settled. So ye've come from home, God pity ye! Go back soon, as soon as ye can, or ye'll never go back at all."

"We're in a hurry, Mrs Dillon," muttered

Dominick impatiently.

"Aren't you happy here?" asked Sally sympathetically.

The old woman frowned.

"Happy, child! I'm old and I'm lonely! How could I be happy? Mebbe, when ye've time, ye'll come in and tell me the news. I never have a letter! No one cares!"

Dominick clattered down the stairs slowly, for all his impatience.

"I will come in," promised Sally. "I'll tell you everything I can. Only now, my brother Dominick is waiting for me!"

The old woman gave her a push.

"Off wid ye! Never keep a lad waiting. They can't stand it! Only when ye've time, on a wet day or when yer brother and sister forget ye're still a stranger and go off and leave ye, come down to me. There'll always be a sup of tay or a cut of bread or, mebbe, cake and me heart's welcome! Remember that—little gerrul from Cork!"

She went in and closed the door. Sally slipped softly down the stairs. She didn't want to talk to any more of the neighbours. She wanted to go out of this house for ever.

Dominick was waiting at the street door.

"That old Mrs Dillon's a terrible one to get

away from," he said. "I know she's lonely and I'm sorry for her. Only I can't stand the miserable way she talks. She grabs Kitty whenever she can. She came here years and years ago to meet someone who never turned up. She hasn't any friends and no one knows how she manages to live!"

"Poor Mrs Dillon!" sighed Sally.

"Cheer up!" said her brother. "Forget Mrs Dillon and remember our job is to buy as much as we can for as little money as possible."

As they came out on the cobble-stones of the Triangle, Sally could scarcely believe it was the same deserted place where the cart had landed her some hours earlier.

The windows were still open but no one looked out at them. The pavements, every inch of space, even the gutters, were crowded with children skipping, playing hopscotch, swinging round the lamp-posts, kicking balls, and even going uneasily up and down on a plank placed across a barrel fixed in the gutter.

A few looked sideways at Sally. Some of the boys nodded a greeting at Dominick.

"Hallo, Irish!" they shouted.

It was a friendly greeting and Dominick waved in reply as they ran through.

He gripped his sister's elbow as they waited

at a crossing for the stream of buses, lorries, motors, carts, cycles to pass.

"Livelier than Cork?" he asked.

Sally considered this.

"There's more of it," she said. "I suppose London is bigger."

Dominick grinned. He was pleased with the answer.

"Sally isn't a slouch," he thought. "I won't have to be explaining her all the time."

Yet when she saw empty stretches of land, with heaps of rubble and, here and there, great square buildings rising into the air, she stopped and clutched his arm.

His eyes followed her pointing finger. Since coming to London he had grown used to the building which went on unceasingly day after day, the changes at school as some children moved out of the district and others came in.

"Do people live there?" asked Sally. "They look like mountains, only there are miles and miles of windows. I don't like them. They're ugly! And there are no trees or gardens."

Dominick blinked. He never bothered about his surroundings, never looked at them. His life was so busy, every moment was occupied. There was no time to consider the shape of buildings, the absence of trees or gardens. All that mattered, he thought, were the people.

Dimly he remembered what he had been told at school.

"There was a great war," he said. "You know, like the ones you read about in the history books. Bombs were dropping out of the sky and knocking the houses flat. Everywhere were piles of stones, bricks and broken tiles. There was nowhere for people to live, so they cleared some of the empty spaces and built up houses as high as they could, so that people could still live in London."

"Those bombs killed people as well as breaking up their homes?" Sally asked.

Her brother nodded.

"Yes, people were killed. I remember the teacher telling us that a whole big city called Coventry had been burned down, all of it. Now they have built it up—a new city! But come on, we mustn't stand here talking all day!"

They came to a wide street filled with stalls. A narrow crowded pathway down the middle slowed the progress of buyers and gazers.

"Could I buy some of the things we want?" asked Sally. "Then we'd be quicker."

Dominick shook his head.

"They wouldn't know what you were asking for. Wait till you talk like other people."

Sally flushed.

She had been wondering why everyone in London talked so strangely; even Kitty and Dominick.

The boy gave her a dig with his elbow.

"You'll soon get used to it. All kinds of people come here. Some can hardly say anything at first. They manage. So will you!"

She trotted meekly behind her brother, marvelling at the way he coaxed a woman to put another tomato in his bag.

"Young sister over to live with us," he explained. "Another mouth to fill!"

The woman looked at Sally with dark melancholy eyes.

"It's hard to leave your own place and you so young," she said kindly. "Never mind. You'll get used to it and—maybe—you'll be happy enough."

Sally tried to keep close to her brother. Soon she forgot him. There was so much to see and so many noises confused her.

She stopped where a row of rabbit hutches, made from wooden boxes with wire netting on one side, were piled on a high, wide wall. The rabbits, ordinary grey and brown ones, were alongside Angoras with long silky coats, nibbling at lettuce leaves and gazing blankly at the passing humans.

Close by were cocks, hens, chickens. The gallant, challenging call of the cocks thrilled Sally as if she were listening to trumpets.

"It's stranger for them than for me," she told herself. "Yet listen to them! They don't care who hears. They're on top of the world!"

Next came the dogs. She put her fingers against the bars which fenced in a mixed group of puppies. She loved dogs only a little less than cats and when each of the six had stood up on its hind legs to give her a friendly lick with a silent appeal to be taken out, she turned to a huddle of Persian kittens, cuddling together for warmth and protection.

"They're like me," she decided. "They're strange and frightened. No! I'm strange but not frightened."

She wandered on. A dark, curly-haired man, wearing a torn, stained white coat, was stirring a sweet, fragrant, steaming mixture in a cauldron over a low flame.

He pulled out a long cord of hot, soft, cough sweet on two sticks, twisted it, doubled it, swung it round and round, then chopped it into small lumps.

He heaped these on an upturned saucepan lid and handed it round to an admiring circle of boys and girls, with a few grown-ups in the background.

He started with Sally. By the time she had finished sucking and chewing her sweet lump, the lid was empty.

"That was lovely!" she declared. "I wish I could make toffee like that!"

He smiled, cut off another piece and held it out to her.

"Here, little stranger! You'll bring me luck!"

"Thank you very much," she said, backing away, without putting the sweet in her mouth.

She wanted to keep it for Dominick and there he was, standing on a high step and gazing anxiously over the market.

"I'm here, Dom! I'm here!" called Sally, waving her lump of cough sweet and squeezing her way towards him.

As she went she was glad to see that the generous cough-sweet seller was handing out sticky bags to a forest of hands holding up coppers and sixpences.

"Did I really make those boys and girls buy his sweets?" she wondered.

Dominick was thankful when she pushed her way up to him.

"Look!" and she handed over the cough sweet she had saved.

"I have an extra tomato and two apples," he boasted. "Now keep with me. We can't spend all our time here. We have to get back. You carry this bag and I'll take the basket. I want sausages, eggs, rashers and butter. We can get the bread and potatoes back in the Triangle and maybe a cauliflower."

Dominick spoke quickly. He had promised Kitty they wouldn't be long and he knew the temptations of the market. Besides, there was so much to be done on Saturday. Always there was the Club where the Irish people for miles around gathered to hear the latest news from home, to sing, dance, make friends and try to imagine they were no longer strangers, emigrants, but in their own country again.

Also Saturday was the day before Sunday. In the Triangle and for many in the streets around, Sunday was an even more crowded day than Saturday. There was church-going, walks, bus rides, for some even exploring London itself.

When Dominick thought of all he had to do, he wanted to hand the basket back to Sally and hurry home.

Clutching the basket he pushed his way steadily towards a shop that was already crowded to the doors.

"Keep close!" he muttered over his shoulder.

Unfortunately Sally heard music coming from higher up the street. Someone was playing a violin and a voice joined in with it.

" 'Danny Boy!' " said Sally.

The market street vanished. She was back on Wise's Hill sitting with Der and Des listening to Paudeen O'Donnell.

"Come along!" called Dominick. "There'll be other Saturdays. Besides old Johnny Doolan will be at the ceilidhe tonight!"

At last they were on their way back, the bag and the basket crammed with their purchases. They waited with the crowd to cross the wide streets, dashed breathlessly across the narrow ones and, there they were, coming into the Triangle.

It was not quite so crowded as before. Most of the children were gathered about a man who was selling plums from a wheelbarrow.

They were big and red. Dominick stopped at once, felt in his pockets and shook his head.

"Now then, youngster," said the man. "Buy a pound of the best plums on the market and take them home to yer mother for her tea!"

The other children turned and looked at Dominick.

"I've only sixpence," he said. "I'll take a

pound of plums for that!"

The man opened his mouth in amazement.

"A pound of the best Kent plums on the market for sixpence!" he exclaimed indignantly. "Trying to be funny, ain't yer?"

The children laughed. One youngster, whizzing by on roller skates, grabbed a plum and darted off, without the man noticing him. The seller was far more interested in Dominick and his offer.

"All right!" said Dominick. "You have plums you want to sell. I have sixpence. Give me sixpenorth of plums! I ought to buy a loaf but I'd sooner have plums."

The man scratched his chin.

"O.K.!" he said at last. "It's a deal!"

He began picking out the smallest, greenest plums he could find.

"I don't want throw-outs!" declared Dominick. "I want the best Kent plums you told me about."

A few women had come out from the doorways to hear the argument.

"Why don't you give the poor kid his plums?" asked a fat woman indignantly. "You wouldn't come here if you could sell your damaged fruit anywhere else."

The fruit seller shrugged his shoulders.

"Come round here!" he ordered Dominick.

The boy obeyed.

"Gimme the sixpence, if you've got it!" said the man.

Dominick handed over six pennies, warm and sticky.

The man laughed and began stuffing plums into the shopping bag.

"Off you go!" he cried.

He gave Dominick a push. The boy and Sally went across the Triangle. At the door they looked back. Women were crowding round the barrow buying plums and, when they looked out from a window, half-way up the stairs, the man was scraping up the last few in his barrow.

"You brought him luck, Dom!" cried Sally enthusiastically. "Just like I did with the cough-sweet man."

"Yes!" agreed Dominick. "Only don't tell Kitty. She doesn't like me to be mixed up with the market. She says it's not dignified!"

9
A London Ceilidhe

hen they climbed to the top of the house and entered the room, Kitty was sitting at the table drawn up by the window. Sheets of paper were spread out there and, to Sally's wonder, her sister was painting a picture.

"How lovely!" she cried, gazing down at twelve pictures, each exactly like the others.

"They're not finished yet," said Kitty. "I hope Mrs Mercer likes them."

Dominick came over to inspect Kitty's work. She looked up at him anxiously.

"What do you think of them, Dom?" she asked. "I've never tried to do a windmill before. I've never even seen one, only in pictures."

Dominick nodded.

"They're good!" he decided. "But you should

have a cow. You're great with cows! And it wouldn't do any harm to throw in some ducks. Everybody likes ducks!"

"I wonder would Mrs Mercer!" murmured Kitty, laying down her brush on a sheet of cardboard beside an open box of paints and a mug of water.

"She's sure to!" said Dominick firmly. "Remember how she praised those swallows you put in the last lot. She always likes birds, when they're extras!"

"I give her more than she pays me for," sighed Kitty. "Only I don't know anyone else who'd buy my pictures. Besides, I like her and I like her shop. I wish she'd take black-and-white drawings. I can draw. I know I can. But I'm not really good at colour!"

"You're wonderful!" cried Sally. "I didn't know I had such a clever sister. You're very good to let me come and live with you and Dom. Only now I am here, please let me do the housework. Mrs Mooney said I was a grand little cook. I can make stew and pancakes, and I can make lovely tea and soup. Really I can!"

Kitty laid down her brush.

"I'm a lucky girl!" she declared. "I don't know anyone else who has such a brother and sister. I believe we're going to be very happy living together. I won't do any more work now because we have to get ready for tonight. I'll put my pictures on the mantelpiece. They'll dry up there and I needn't do another stroke of work till Monday!"

"You won't forget the ducks!" Dominick reminded her.

Kitty spread her pictures on the mantelpiece.

"Now we'll unpack your bag," she told Sally. "Your blue frock isn't too bad. But where are your best shoes?"

"I haven't any," Sally confessed, looking down mournfully at the strong lace boots she was wearing.

Kitty bit her thumb. She was thinking hard.

"I know!" she said at last. "You can wear a pair of my shoes. We'll stuff the toes with paper to make them fit you! Your frock will need ironing. Here we are!" She opened the big double cupboard which stood against the wall and took out a pair of buckle shoes.

Sally tried them on.

"They're a bit big. Poke this piece of newspaper in the toes and they'll be a perfect fit!" declared Kitty. "Give them a rub while I'm ironing your frock. Look! The boot brushes and polish are under the sink."

"Give the shoes to me!" demanded Dominick. "I'm the shoe cleaner here. Don't they have dances on Wise's Hill? I thought people in Ireland never stopped dancing and singing."

"The Mooneys were poor," explained Sally. "Even Janey had to give up competing at the Feis because she hadn't the shoes or the dress. And she was a marvel at dancing. She won seven medals!"

"Wouldn't you think someone would pay for her shoes?" asked Kitty indignantly.

"Nobody knew!" Sally told her. "The Mooneys were proud. Janey just pretended she was tired of dancing."

Kitty shook out the folds of the blue frock.

"It's terrible short!" sighed Sally. "I'm really too big for it."

Kitty laughed.

"That won't matter! Look! Here's a necklace and a ribbon for your hair. With them and a pair of my stockings you'll look grand. Wash your face and hands. I'll fix your hair. Dom! Put on your best suit and take a clean hanky!"

At last they were ready. Kitty switched off the light, made sure the key was in her purse and there they were, out on the stairs, groping their way down. From one room they could hear the radio giving the weather report. In another the whole family were having a noisy argument. On a lower floor a baby was crying. Mrs Dillon looked out from her door and wished them a happy evening.

"I thought you'd be glad of the light," she said. "Them stairs are terrible dark and dangerous. Wouldn't you think the Government would give us a glimmer to find our way!"

She looked so pale and forlorn Kitty was sorry for her.

"Why don't you come with us, Mrs Dillon?" she asked. "I'll treat you to a ticket. There'll be singing and music as well as the dancing. And all the people will be from Ireland. You'd enjoy that!"

The little woman laughed—a queer crackling noise like the rustle of dry leaves blown by the winter wind.

"I'd look nice among a crowd of lively young people," she said. "They'd think ye were bringing a banshee along wid ye. Still an all, I thank ye for the kind thought!"

She went in and closed her door, leaving them in a darkness which seemed deeper than before.

Holding on to the banisters, they went slowly down, Dominick first, then Kitty. Last of all came Sally, treading very carefully because of the light, easy-fitting shoes which made her feel she could fly.

"Thank goodness I won't be a show in boys' boots," she thought.

Then she was ashamed. Hadn't Mrs Mooney had to save and scrape to buy those boots?

Sally knew ingratitude was the worst sin of all. She felt hot and uncomfortable. "It's terrible hard to be good," she murmured.

They had reached the front door. Dominick flung it open and out they went, slamming it behind them.

There were three street lamps in the Triangle, one at each corner, and three groups were gathered about them, one playing cards, one singing and the third group—the largest—just talking.

"Where are you off to?" called a girl as they passed.

"To the dance!" answered Kitty.

"Best leave the kids at home and take me," said a lanky youth with a grin.

"Kids!" muttered Dominick impatiently. "I'm no kid!"

Sally didn't mind being called a kid. Her hand was clasped in Kitty's. She felt happy and excited.

Now they came out on the big wide road

Dominick and herself had crossed earlier in the day. The pavements were even more crowded than before and they had to move slowly to avoid being separated.

There were shops on both sides. These were open and people squeezed into them while others stared in at the windows. Along the pavement edge were stalls where fruit, vegetables, sweets, books, toys, chipped potatoes, pickled cucumbers, cockles and whelks were being sold.

In between the stalls were men and women who sang, played violins, guitars, mouth-organs. Others preached loudly and two groups were singing hymns.

Sally was so interested in all this she forgot they were on their way to a ceilidhe until Kitty pushed her across the pavement towards a dark narrow turning.

"We're there!" Dominick told Sally.

"Almost!" added Kitty.

They came to a hall, not very large, with a wide open door. Music and the sound of many voices came to them. Kitty pulled out a purse from her coat pocket and laid down her money on a table at the door.

"There's three of us, Mr Finnegan!" she said. "This is Sally, my little sister from Cork."

The young man, sitting at the table, smiled.

"A hundred thousand welcomes!" he said, nodding at Sally.

"The latest arrival from Cork!" he added. "Welcome! May you go back soon. We've a distinguished visitor from your city here this evening. He's on his way to play in a dozen big cities in Europe before going to America. Aren't we the lucky ones tonight? Perhaps you've heard him play before?"

He pointed to the end of the hall. Sally was thrilled. Could there be anyone else just over from Cork? Someone she knew?

A tall dark man with a violin under his arm was standing beside a piano on the platform. The girl sitting on the piano stool was looking up at him with a delighted smile.

Sally shook her head so that the blue ribbon Kitty had tied so carefully round her hair slipped down and hung about her neck.

"No! I've never seen him or heard him either," she said regretfully, thinking of the old fiddler who played on Wise's Hill every Sunday night. Mr Mooney had told Sally that the fiddler had divided the city into seven parts and visited each district in turn.

He was a thin ragged man who, on wet or cold nights, wrapped his coat round his violin and went shivering in his shirt-sleeves. He didn't play very well but he played for the children dancing and gave the grown-ups the tunes they liked.

Sally frowned at the man standing by the piano. Poor Johnny Doolan would have been too shy to talk to him—he looked so grand. He had never played in the street! She was sure of that!

"Will he play for the dancing or is that beneath him?" asked Kitty.

The young man carefully piled the money lying on the table into little heaps.

"John Hogan says he offered to play for the dancing and singing and anything else we like. He's a grand man and a fine musician. They do say he takes his fiddle to bed with him.

"Now you two young ones go along and take your places for the children's sixteen-handed reel. We start with that tonight!"

Sally hung back.

"I'll wait!" she said.

"And waste my best shoes!" cried Kitty. "Take her along, Dom! A ceilidhe isn't any fun at all if you don't dance."

The other children were lining up and the moment the musician from Cork began tuning his fiddle Sally forgot her shyness. How glad she was Janey had taught her to dance. When the music started she was sure she would be as good as the others and so she was.

By the time she was standing against the wall listening to "The Harp that Once" she was wondering would she have another chance.

The girl standing beside her was a chatterbox.

"Dom says you'll be in my class at school. Shall I ask if you can sit next to me? My name's Marcella Lanigan. Your hair ribbon's fallen down. Shall I fix it for you?"

"Yes, please!" answered Sally, replying to her last question.

They stood against the wall, Marcella proud to tell how many people she knew. Sally listened in a daze. Suddenly she started. "Wasn't that tall dark woman in a flowered silk frock Mrs Regan of the *Wave of Tory*?"

For a moment she was back in the warm dry cabin of the little ship, safe and snug, hidden away from fog and storms. And she had almost forgotten the kindness and friendliness she had found there. She stepped forward, not daring to look away for fear that gay smiling face would vanish.

Marcella grabbed her arm.

"You mustn't do that! You nearly knocked into a dancer."

Sally tried to explain.

"There's a friend over there. I must speak with her. She's from the ship, the *Wave of Tory*!"

"I'll come too! Someone must keep you from bumping into everyone. Follow me and keep away from the centre."

They were only half-way round when Mrs Regan saw them. She waved a newspaper she was holding as if it were a banner of triumph. Sally, shaking off Marcella's hand, darted towards her.

Mrs Regan held out her arms.

"So here's my little emigrant!" she cried. "Captain! Captain! Will ye look who's here! Sally Nolan from Cork. And haven't they smartened ye up? Where's the sister and the brother? Captain! Do ye remember the young ones we brought over in the fog? This is the best chess player ye ever carried!"

Sally looked round and there was the Captain, bareheaded, a pipe in his mouth, no longer giving orders or troubling about his ship but taking a holiday on land and enjoying the ceilidhe as much as anyone there.

"How's the chess going?" he asked. "You'll play a game with me when you're coming back."

Smiling broadly he held out a strong brown hand. Sally was delighted. Here she was among friends and home did not seem far away.

Her eyes sparkled and the dancers, as they whirled by, smiled at her animation. Some of the younger ones looked curiously at this dark-eyed girl with her hair in her eyes and the ribbon still hanging about her neck.

The violinist from Cork came up on the platform and played "Danny Boy," "I'll Take You Home Again, Kathleen," "The Castle of Dromore" and all the other melodies the exiles loved. Everyone in the hall sang the choruses.

Sally could imagine that old Johnny Doolan, the fiddler she had heard so often, playing on Wise's Hill was up there too playing with him. She knew that the older people in the hall were remembering Cork or Dublin—all the places they came from, just as she was doing.

Next came refreshments. They had thick ham sandwiches and cups of hot strong tea. They listened to more singing and recitations. The violinist played again till even Marcella stood motionless and silent.

There was more dancing. There were farewells and promises of future meetings. Then Sally was walking home in the moonlight between Kitty and Dominick, thinking that the stars were as bright and lovely here as they were in Cork.

10
A Strange School

ally was beginning to feel that she had passed most of her life in the Triangle when one Sunday night Kitty, who was pouring tea while Dominick buttered the hot toast, announced suddenly:

"School starts tomorrow, Sally! Sister Agnes knows all about you. Give her this note. You'll be in Miss O'Grady's class and you can go along with Dom. He'll introduce you. I wish I could come but I mustn't be late at the shop."

Sally had known she would have to go to school some time. Each day it had come nearer and nearer. She had tried not to think about school, and life had become so gay and exciting she had almost succeeded.

Now the holidays were over. She sighed so deeply Kitty looked alarmed, but Dominick laughed.

"You'll be a heroine for a day—the latest arrival from Ireland!"

"There's your new school-bag," said Kitty consolingly. "With your new blue frock, your brown shoes and stockings, you'll be one of the smartest girls at the Guardian Angels! That does help, you know."

Sally looked at her sister's face.

"Kitty's really hoping you'll be the cleverest girl in the school!" Dominick spluttered through a mouthful of bread, butter and marmalade.

"Don't you like going to school?" asked Kitty. "I think I did."

She tried to look back to her life when she was only Sally's age—six years ago.

"I'm sure I did," she added, "only it's so long back, I almost forget, though I have a very pleasant feeling about that school in Cork."

"I hated it," said Sally, "but it wasn't the school's fault. It was mine. I was nearly always late and sometimes I didn't go at all. There was such a lot to do at home and Mrs Mooney thought schooling didn't matter for girls."

Kitty shook her head in bewilderment.

"It does, you know!" she said. "It matters for everybody!"

***

"Time!" announced Dominick, glancing at the clock on the mantelpiece. "Come along, Sally! And don't be scared. They can't eat you!"

"Good luck!" called Kitty from the door.

"Safe home, ye poor scrap!" whispered old Mrs Dillon, poking out her head.

Now they were in the Triangle. From every doorway boys and girls were running off to school. Some went proudly, conscious of clean hands, well-brushed hair, shining shoes and a school-bag packed with books.

Others were just finishing breakfast, taking hurried bites at slices of bread and butter or jam as they went along, though fully aware that jammy hands and faces were not welcomed at morning school.

A few darted back suddenly for something they had forgotten—a clean handkerchief, a pen, a pencil or a school-book, then rushed on hoping they would not be too late.

Among the others were the untidy children, with shabby or ragged clothes, old shoes, torn socks and no books. These kicked a would-be careless and defiant way along the gutter.

Sally, glancing at these unfortunates and recalling how, not long ago, she was of their company, felt a pang of sympathy.

Only for Kitty she would still be one of them.

Now, because her sister was kind and clever, she would enter a new school in new clothes, a credit to everyone!

"I must try to be the cleverest girl in the school," she thought desperately. "Only I'm not clever at all!"

Dominick pranced along beside her, shouting greetings to friends as they emerged from other houses.

They reached the main road.

"Let's rush it and be there first!" suggested the boy.

He was out of breath before Sally realized they were running.

"You can run!" he panted admiringly.

"I did win a prize for running!" Sally told him. "It's the only prize I ever did win!"

"Be reasonable!" pleaded Dominick. "You can't win every prize."

They reached the school feeling pleased with one another.

A group of girls in the open gateway stared at Dominick as he entered.

"The boys' school is along there," a big girl told him haughtily, waving her arm. "Can't you read? It says Girls' School here!"

"So it does!" retorted Dominick. "But I only wanted a look. No harm in looking, is there?"

Sally giggled. She forgot to be nervous as they went into a large hall where a nun in blue and white, and a group of teachers, were receiving parents and new pupils.

"Pity I'm not taller," whispered Dom. "I could pretend to be your father."

This time Sally didn't laugh, for the group at the end of the hall were watching them with interest. Dominick strode forward and handed Kitty's note to Sister Agnes, the nun in charge.

"My sister Kitty sent the note," he said, pulling Sally forward. "This is my other sister!"

"Your little sister!" said the nun. "You're very welcome, dear! I hope you'll be happy with us."

"I'm not really a little sister," Sally tried to explain but nobody listened.

"This is Sally Nolan from Cork," said Sister Agnes to the teachers, as she read the note. "And this is Dominick. Well, Dominick, you can run off to your own school now. We'll take care of your little sister."

"So long, Sally!" said Dominick, rushing back down the hall.

This time Sally was determined to explain.

"I'm not really Dom's little sister," she declared. "I'm more than a year older than he is."

Still no one took any notice, for Marcella

Lanigan, who was the centre of a group of girls, saw Sally and came over.

"I know Sally," she told Sister Agnes. "Please may we sit together?"

The nun nodded.

"A very good idea if Miss O'Grady has no objection!"

Miss O'Grady was a tall, handsome girl with flashing eyes and curly red hair. She had an air of great good humour.

"She'll agree to anything," whispered Marcella.

"Why not?" asked Miss O'Grady cheerfully. "If I make Marcella responsible for Sally I have two girls less to bother about!"

The other girls were looking on curiously. Marcella pulled Sally by the arm over to the group.

"All my friends can be yours!" she told Sally generously.

Just then the bell began to ring. The girls formed up in lines and Sally had time to look round.

The more she looked, the bigger her eyes grew. She was puzzled.

"This is a very strange school!" she thought. But she did not venture to ask Marcella about it. She knew enough of schools to understand that talking was not allowed while the classes were arranging themselves.

In the Cork school the children mostly belonged to the city. A few came from outside, one was from Connemara and half a dozen from scattered towns along the coast.

Here, as well as the London girls and the strangers from Ireland, there were, to Sally's amazement, children with yellow faces and dark slanting eyes. Others had brown, chocolate-coloured skin while two were quite black with shining curls, merry dancing eyes and beautiful white teeth.

"This is a very strange school!" thought Sally again. "But I like it."

11
Living in London

n Cork Sally had very little chance to make friends at school. She had to bring Des and Der in the morning and take them home again. She helped with the cooking, cleaning and marketing.

The other girls played ball or skipped. Sally had no ball or rope and was too proud to use the playthings belonging to others even if she had had the time.

When Mr Mooney remembered his own young days he would give her a penny, a threepenny-bit or a sixpence. Once he had given her a shilling. But the Mooneys had no toys.

Now she was one of the neatest and best-dressed girls at the Guardian Angels' School. She had a whole shilling every Saturday morning and as good a lunch to pack in her satchel as any girl in her class.

Her brother was with the best hurlers and footballers in the boys' school. He sang in the church choir and played in the school fife and drum band. So she had something to boast about.

Unfortunately Sally was the worst at spelling and arithmetic in her class. Even the children from Asia and Africa, who were forgiven a great many blunders because they were learning lessons in a language strange to them, were better than Sally.

If it hadn't been for her memory she would have been in absolute disgrace. She had a wonderful memory. She could recite long poems, remember dates, names of rivers, towns, historical characters and happenings.

Marcella Lanigan comforted her.

"If you can remember those awful old dates and people who were dead long before we were born, you've nothing to worry about. You prompt me and I'll prompt you. Thanks be, I'm good at arithmetic and spelling."

Sally looked worried.

"Isn't prompting as bad as cheating?" she asked.

"And whose fault is that?" demanded Marcella cheerfully. "Do we want to learn all those horrid lessons? It's the people who make us do it who are really to blame, not us!"

Sally wasn't convinced. But she hated arguing, so said no more.

She wanted to help Kitty all she could so, with her friend Marcella, she joined the cookery class.

"My mother says it's more important for a girl to be a good cook than to play the violin or the piano," Marcella told Sally.

"I'd love to play the violin," said Sally. "Just think of standing up in the Club with all the people clapping and admiring your playing. I'd sooner that than anything else. I'd love to do something with my fingers!"

"Sewing? Knitting?" asked Marcella scornfully.

Sally shook her head. Her eyes were dreaming.

"No! I don't mean that!"

"Learn to make jam roll and everyone will think you're a marvel!" chuckled Marcella. "Anybody can play around with plasticine if that's what you mean. Modelling is a game for babies. After all, Sally, you're not in the kindergarten!"

They both laughed.

The two girls were happy at the cookery

lessons, but Sally found her greatest pleasure in moulding the dough into strange shapes.

She was delighted when she was able to cook a Sunday dinner which Kitty said was the best she had ever eaten.

"Isn't this better than playing the violin?" demanded Dominick, his mouth full.

Sally was proud of her cooking but she shook her head.

"I'd sooner play the violin, or sing, or maybe paint like Kitty," she said. "Still, I'm not sure!"

"I wish you could paint," her sister told her. "We could take turns at trying to do something really good. We'll go to the National Gallery today. We can get there on the bus. You'll see some wonderful pictures. Will you come, Dom, or are you going to the park?"

Dominick swaggered across the room.

"You don't suppose I'd let you two girls go to Trafalgar Square by yourselves, do you? Besides, I gave my ankle a twist yesterday and I must be careful for a few days. I hope I'll be chosen to play in the big school match."

"Oh Dom! That would be fine!" said Kitty, jumping up. "We'll come and clap!"

"Can Marcella come with us?" asked Sally. "She'd love to come and she's been a good friend to me."

"Of course she can!" said Kitty. "I like Marcella. Why don't you ask her to tea—if you think the place is good enough."

Sally looked around at the room and thought of the big, crowded, untidy home of the Mooneys on Wise's Hill. Once she had thought that must be the snuggest and most comfortable home in the world. Now she knew the best of it was the people who lived there. She would never forget the Mooneys. Never! Would she ever see them again?

"Well?" asked Kitty, waiting for her response. "Is the Nolan establishment grand enough for Miss Marcella?"

Sally blinked.

"I had forgotten. I was remembering Wise's Hill. Marcella will think this wonderful. I've told her about your pictures and the ships beyond the window and all about Dom. You'll like Marcella!"

"Do I have to comb my hair and wash my hands in honour of the Princess Marcella?" asked Dominick. "Mind you, we've seen her at the Club. Only don't ask her till I am chosen for the team. I may not be. There are lots of other boys. Some of them are real good. There's one they call the little Stepney Wonder! And I'm a month older than he is!"

"I won't say a word until you tell me to," promised Sally.

They went to the National Gallery in Trafalgar Square. Sally thought what a pity it was that London should be so big.

"If I had my way," she said, "I'd throw away the long straggly streets where there are hundreds and hundreds of ugly houses all the same. I'd make a wonderful city with the docks, the river, the bridges, the parks and the squares!"

"And where would the people live?" asked Kitty.

"I didn't mean to speak out loud," Sally told her. "I was really thinking to myself."

The fountains were playing in Trafalgar Square, with the massive lions and the slender column in the centre. Kitty wished she had the time and the talent to paint a picture of it all—the square, the people, the pigeons and the whole animated scene.

Sally stood admiring the lions even while they fed the pigeons. Only for Dominick's impatience the gallery would have been closed before they reached the doors.

"It's bigger than the gallery in Cork!" decided Sally. "Mr Mooney took me and Janey there one day. We saw a wonderful picture of men with guns at the top of the staircase and he could tell us the name of every one of them!"

"One day you'll really have to tell us about Cork," said Kitty. "I'm ashamed but I've almost forgotten it."

"If we were told we could go back there tomorrow, what would you do?" asked Dominick, his head on one side.

Kitty gasped, recovered and gave him a push.

"What nonsense you talk!" she cried.

"Oh! My poor foot! I'm destroyed!" lamented the boy, pretending to limp. "I'll never be chosen to play in the match!"

Kitty clutched his arm.

"Dom! Did I hurt you? I am sorry. I'd never forgive myself if you lost the match through my fault."

He laughed and ran up the steps, waiting at the top, for the crowds of the world were streaming up there. Hurrying visitors found their passage slowed by the revolving doors.

A boy who had forced his way through found himself alone and tried to go back to his friends. Dominick was ahead of his sisters and, pushing vigorously, found he could not move because the other boy was pushing against him.

Some of the crowd laughed. Others were annoyed at the delay, for they were in a hurry to see the paintings.

"Boys shouldn't be allowed in the gallery," snapped one man indignantly. "They always get up to tricks!"

The two boys, pushing in opposite directions, were stuck.

"Now you can't stay there," said the man in charge, "though a night in the gallery would teach you both a lesson!"

Dominick and the other boy looked at one another angrily. Neither would give way.

Dom's sisters were becoming anxious when a tall man leaned forward, gripped him by the shoulders, and pulled him out.

The other boy pushed through triumphantly and clattered down the steps away from the gallery.

The tall man, still gripping Dominick, propelled him through the revolving doors. He found himself inside.

"Thank you, sir!" he stammered.

"Good thing some youngsters have manners even if they've no sense!" said the attendant gruffly.

Yet he smiled at Dom.

"Everybody likes Dom!" whispered Kitty to her sister. "The man who pushed him through is still looking at him!"

Sally glanced back. The man was still standing there, unconscious of the people pushing against him. She was sure it wasn't Dom he was looking at but Kitty.

His eyes were puzzled and bewildered as if he could not believe what he saw.

They turned into a side room where Kitty had caught sight of a sudden blaze of colour. Sally looked back. The man was moving slowly, peering into every face.

"He wants to see us again!" she thought. "But he doesn't know where we've gone."

She touched her sister's arm.

"I think that man is looking for us," she whispered. "Shall we go back?"

Kitty laughed and shook her head.

"Of course not! We can't make friends with any stranger we meet in a picture gallery. Besides, it's quite likely you're mistaken. He may be an artist just interested in faces. Oh, Sally! If only I could really paint! Look! Look! That picture is alive!"

She stopped in front of a picture of "The Adoration" by an Italian artist, a vision in delicate blue and gold.

On the way out Sally stood looking down at the pictures in tessellated tiles over which the hurrying feet of so many visitors to the gallery passed indifferently.

She saw an angel bending compassionately over a dying girl. Next she stood on the figure of a man defying the Devil. Before she could examine the others Dominick pulled her away towards the revolving doors.

"We never properly looked at the place," he grumbled. "One day I'm coming early and I'll see every picture, if I have to stay all night."

Near the entrance he paused to look at a statue of two men wrestling.

"I like that," he said. "Those two know what they're doing!"

"I wish I could be more help to Kitty!" Sally said to herself. "She can paint and she'd do better if she had more time. When we go home I'll get the tea ready. I won't let her lift a finger. I could even cook some pancakes."

She did make pancakes, light, thin and golden brown, spread with strawberry jam and then rolled up. She made two dozen. They ate them in their fingers and not one was left.

Indeed Dominick picked up the dish in which Sally had mixed the batter and sighed when he discovered that every bit had been scraped out. Only the appetizing smell remained. They were so good Sally decided to make some the day Marcella came to tea.

Sally washed up, Dominick dried and Kitty sat in an armchair drawn up to the window.

"That's a picture I'd love to paint!" she said, pointing through the window to a battered little steamer where a man leaned against the side smoking, a dog stretched at his feet.

"Shall I bring your book and paints and brushes?" asked Sally eagerly.

Kitty shook her head.

"No! I'll finish my work. Mrs Mercer is waiting for it. Besides, she doesn't care for ships and I can't do them very well. Sometimes I'm sure I'm no good at all! That's the way I feel tonight!

"Seeing all those wonderful paintings has made me know the truth about myself. It's better to make good pancakes than paint poor pictures. You stick to cooking, Sally!"

"Maybe I will!" said Sally.

12
The Hurling Match

arcella Lanigan met Dominick and his sisters at the Irish Club on the day of the junior hurling match. Dominick was with the other players receiving last-minute instructions from the trainer.

Marcella wished she had a brother young enough to play with the junior team or old enough to be with the seniors. Her three brothers were in between and they had no interest in hurling or in football.

One was a champion swimmer. One collected rare and strange plants. The eldest had only one interest—the theatre. He saved his pocket money to see new plays, old plays, any kind of plays.

Ronan Lanigan was seventeen and he couldn't make up his mind whether he would be a great actor, a great dramatist or a great producer. He was determined to be great in some way or other so long as it had to do with the theatre.

In Cork Sally was always hearing of young ones who wanted to get a regular job in the civil service, to go to America or England. She had known Johnny Doolan the fiddler, Paudeen O'Donnell the ballad singer, as well as fruit and fish sellers, carpenters and washer-women. But they were old and settled. She found it thrilling to meet people who hoped one day to be famous.

"London is so big!" Kitty told her. "Anything could happen here. Every day quite ordinary people wake up and find themselves suddenly rich and famous."

"Yet they want to go back where they belong, don't they?" Sally asked. "If you were rich enough you'd go back to Cork, wouldn't you?"

Kitty didn't answer. Sally was alarmed.

"You wouldn't want never to go back home any more?" she pleaded. "Fancy being an emigrant all your life. That would be terrible!"

Here in the Irish Club on the day of the hurling match no one thought of the time when it might be possible to go back home to Ireland, least of all the boys in the team who were straining every nerve to show how good they could be. Tonight and tomorrow they would be singing songs of lament, of sorrow at parting from their native land and of longing to go back. But now everyone was caught up with the excitement of the coming match.

The sun shone, a light wind blew. The pipers' band formed up and, playing "Let Erin Remember," marched out of the hall to lead the throng.

The hurling team came close behind and—trying to keep in time with the music—the rest of the people, men, women and children, streamed from the hall. It was a great thrill for them.

Yet the Londoners, crowding the pavements, stared indifferently. There was so much to see, so much to do. The moment the band and its followers passed out of sight they were forgotten.

Kitty held Sally's hand in hers. Marcella was on the other side.

"Keep with me!" whispered Kitty. "We may get a chance of squeezing into the same bus as Dom. Doesn't he look fine! He's the best hurler for his age in the team!"

Most of the time Sally couldn't see her brother. Only when the band turned a corner did she catch a glimpse of him—red-faced, serious and determined, very neat in his dark pants and green-striped jersey.

She was proud of him. When she looked up at Kitty and saw her soft curly hair, her sparkling eyes and smiling lips she felt prouder still.

"Thanks be, I've decent clothes and shoes," she thought. "I won't disgrace the family!"

She caught sight of herself in a long narrow glass which reflected them all one after the other.

She was startled at what she saw.

"I don't look too bad after all!" she decided.

The band stopped. The team stopped. Their followers spread over the pavement and there were three double-decker buses waiting for them.

Marcella saw her looking into the mirror and laughed.

"That's what I do!" she said. "I love seeing myself as I go along the street!"

"Come along, you two!" called Mr Finnegan, the young man who had welcomed Sally on her first visit to the Club. "Make way for Dom's two sisters! Oh! Is this your friend? We'll squeeze her in too!"

Some of the team went inside but Dominick scrambled on top where his sisters sat.

"Let's sit at the back," Kitty told Sally,

pulling her down to the next seat. Marcella sat beside them. "It's only fair to let the boys and the band have the front seats. It's their day of glory!"

Sally didn't mind where she sat if she could be with Kitty and Marcella. It was a grand bus and the seats were very comfortable. The streets weren't so crowded today and most of the people were sauntering along the pavements looking very leisurely and contented with themselves. They were all dressed in their Sunday best.

Kitty leaned forward.

"Enjoying yourself?" she asked.

"I am! I am!" cried Sally.

"I love bus rides!" declared Marcella.

Everyone on the bus was talking so hard no one took any notice.

"I thought I didn't like crowds," reflected Sally. "But when they're good-tempered and you feel good in yourself it's nice to be in a crowd."

"I've never been on such a long bus ride before!" she told Marcella. "It must have been wonderful in the days when people travelled in stage-coaches drawn by horses. I'd love that, wouldn't you?"

"I suppose I would!" replied Marcella a little

doubtfully. "Only it must have been very slow!"

They had left the crowded streets behind them. The bus swung out on a wide common, slowed down and came to a stop.

In a moment the skirl of the pipes rose again in the air. Idlers came running across the grass and, by the time Kitty, Sally and Marcella were able to follow the band and the team, a cheerful, noisy crowd surrounded them.

"There's a camogie team for girls in London," said Kitty. "I suppose you learned to play in Cork?"

Sally shook her head.

"Do you play camogie?" she ventured.

"I never had the time or the chance," her sister told her. "I've been too busy with work. And I've always liked dancing better than games."

"I wouldn't play camogie if I had the chance!" Marcella confessed. "But my sister loves it. She'd sooner play camogie than go swimming! Can you swim, Sally?"

"I can't and I'm no good at games!" Sally told her friend.

The other hurling team had brought their crowd of supporters with them, and before the game started friends from different corners of London were greeting one another.

"There must be nearly as many Irish people in London as there are English," said Sally.

Kitty laughed.

"Where I work I hardly ever see anyone from Ireland," she answered. "There are French, Germans, Austrians, Italians and heaps of Americans. But I've only seen about half a dozen Irish away from the Club and the church."

"Where do you work?" Sally asked her.

"In a place near Soho on the other side of London," Kitty answered. "It's called Mercer's Curio Shop. Mrs Mercer keeps it and I help. She sells my pictures there. But her real trade is in jewellery and embroidery, antique furniture and that kind of thing. One day when we're not too busy I'll take you there!"

A sudden roar went up round the field.

"Look! Look!" cried Kitty. "There's Dom after the ball! See how he lifts it on his stick! Isn't he a grand player!"

Dominick was carrying the ball down the field to the tumultuous cheers of the crowd.

Marcella was even more excited than Dominick's sisters. She clapped, cheered, jumped up and down with as much enthusiasm as anyone.

"I think I'll change my mind and join my

sister's camogie team. It's just as good as hurling! People who play hockey and baseball don't know about our Irish games which are just as fine."

"I'd sooner swim and row!" Sally told Marcella.

They discussed games while they watched the hurling match. Both sides were so evenly matched that neither could win. At one time it looked as if Dominick's team would be victorious, for he succeeded in getting the ball up the field and scored a goal.

All the supporters from the Irish Club went wild then and the girls were delighted. But later the opponents equalized with another goal. So at the finish the match would have to be replayed. In spite of their disappointment at not winning everyone agreed it had been a great game.

On the way back Dominick travelled with the girls. They had to leave him at the Club, for he was entertained to tea with the other players.

13
Marcella Comes to Tea

arcella's father was a doctor, and the family lived in a big imposing house in Commercial Road. There was a shining brass plate on the door and all the windows had long lace curtains.

Yet she was thrilled at the strange atmosphere which belonged to the Triangle. She liked the way the inhabitants sat on their doorsteps or at the window-sills or grouped themselves around the street lamps.

She liked climbing the dark narrow staircase and, when she arrived in the big room with its wide window, looking out upon sails and funnels of ships, she envied Sally.

"All we can see from our windows are lines and lines of houses," she complained. "This is romantic! If I lived here I'd climb out of the window one night and stow away on that ship."

"The first time I looked out there, a monkey chattered at me!" Sally told her.

"This is like a pirates' den!" cried Marcella. "Kitty! If Sally goes back to Cork will you let me come and live with you?"

"Perhaps I will!" Kitty answered, laughing.

Sally was very quiet. As they were coming away from the hurling field she had seen the man who helped Dom at the picture gallery, wedged in the crowd waiting for a bus.

He was staring at the boy so curiously that she was very puzzled. Who was he? Had he known Dominick before and did he want to speak to him again? But at the picture gallery it was at Kitty he looked.

His sad eyes haunted her. She wished she knew what he was thinking of and how she could help him.

Kitty glanced at Sally and saw her thoughts were far away.

"Always dreaming!" she said. "What is it now, Sally?"

Sally smiled.

"I'm not dreaming," she answered. "I was thinking about that man who pulled Dom out of the turning doors at the picture gallery. You remember, Kitty?"

Kitty nodded.

"He was at the match today and he watched Dom all the time. At the picture gallery it was at you he looked!"

"I don't suppose he'd ever seen such wonderful people before," laughed Marcella. "Next time he'll be studying you, Sally!"

"You imagined it all!" said Kitty. "Or if it did happen it was just that helping Dom at the picture gallery made him notice us again. He may be an Irishman stranded in London and lonely for his own people. It often happens. He may turn up at the Club one Saturday. And then we shall hear all about him!"

"Oh Kitty! You have destroyed Sally's mystery!" cried Marcella. "She'll never forgive you!"

"Now for tea!" said Kitty. "The kettle's boiling!"

Over tea Marcella told them stories of her father and his career as a doctor. He had started in two rooms over a marine store, down by the docks where seamen came to buy oilskins, chests, jerseys, rope-ladders and all kinds of ships' gear.

He had treated his first case there—a man who had stumbled into a ship's hold when he came aboard in the dark. He had attended

Chinese, Japanese and Malay seamen. In the dock district he had treated men of all colours and every nationality, seafarers from merchant ships, yachts, from tugs and barges and he had learned something from each one of them.

"That must have been a wonderful life!" said Kitty. "But a terrible one. Just think of having to deal with all those sick people."

"It's a great life!" declared Marcella. "That's the life I want!"

Kitty and Sally looked at her with admiration.

"You want to be a nurse?" asked Kitty.

"No!" answered Marcella proudly. "I want to be a doctor!"

Kitty held out her hand.

"May you have your wish!" she said.

They shook hands solemnly.

"And I wish you all the luck in the world!" added Sally, remembering the favourite wish of Wise's Hill.

"I'll make another pot of tea!" announced Kitty.

They had finished the sandwiches. Now they started on the lemon-cheese tart which Kitty had bought at the baker's round the corner. She wished that Dom was with them, not only to share the sandwiches—chopped boiled beef mixed with tomato sauce—but so that he could listen to Marcella.

"My young brother is ambitious too," she told Marcella. "He wants to be the best hurler in London."

"May he have his wish!" Marcella lifted her cup of tea.

The other two joined her, laughing.

"Now tell me, what do you want to be?" she asked Kitty. "Sally's told me all the things you can do. She thinks you're a marvel. So do I. But what is the special thing you want most of all?"

Kitty flushed.

"I always wanted to be an artist, and when Mrs Mercer took the pictures I painted and sold them in her shop, I thought I really was one."

"So you are!" declared Sally.

Kitty shook her head. But she was pleased with Sally's praise.

"Even when I saw fine pictures displayed in shops I was silly enough to think mine were every bit as good. But that Sunday when we went to the National Gallery something happened to me. It was as if I'd been wearing dark glasses and had just taken them off. I felt I had never seen colour or design before. I knew then I wasn't an artist."

She sat silent, leaning back in her chair, her

eyes cast down.

Kitty was so sad that Sally felt tears of sympathy welling up. She couldn't speak.

"Perhaps you became an artist then," said Marcella. "Before that you just dabbed paint on paper. Children can do that. A real artist has to know more, feel more and understand more."

Sally gazed at Marcella in bewilderment. Was this her gay, noisy friend, who was always joking and teasing, and who had once declared that her one ambition was to be a good cook?

"I always liked her," Sally told herself. "But I never really knew her. I'm glad she's my friend!"

Kitty looked up.

"Thank you, Marcella," she said. "I hope you're right!"

Just then Dominick came in.

Kitty had saved a plate of sandwiches and a wedge of lemon-cheese tart for him. He had eaten as much as any of the other boys at the Club tea but he was quite ready for more.

His big sister made a fresh pot of tea for him. Marcella poured it out and Sally just sat admiring him as he retold every blow struck in the hurling match that day.

He took a long drink of hot tea, crammed a sandwich into his mouth, jumped up, seized a broom and explained his best stroke—the one that should have won the match.

Kitty took the broom from him.

"You sit down and rest," she said. "We're all proud of you and we'll be prouder still when you win the next match and teach that stuck-up Wimbledon crowd a lesson!"

"Ah, they're not bad fellas!" Dom declared. "They play fair. And they treated our team to whacking great ice-cream wafers, strawberry, chocolate and vanilla!"

"Oo!" exclaimed Sally.

"You weren't around or I'd have saved some for you," said Dom generously. "They were better than we had at the Club," he declared, "though they weren't bad either," he added, remembering his manners.

14
Sally's Jam Tart

very Sunday the young Nolans made expeditions beyond the Triangle. Because they hadn't much money they walked as far as they could, only taking the bus to reach home again.

Some of the neighbours had told Kitty about Chinatown and, because she had read stories about China, she was determined to show Sally something she could never see in Cork.

"Men with pigtails," she said. "They wear robes and shuffle along like this!"

She tucked her arms into her sleeves and shuffled across the room. Her brother and sister watched eagerly.

"The women"—she paused—"I don't know about them. Of course they're beautiful and slant-eyed and wear embroidered robes of silk."

"They never came this way!" declared Dominick.

"I think I saw them my first day here," Sally told Kitty, looking very thoughtful.

She walked over and gazed out. The other two rushed to the window.

A black-and-white dog trotted across the bridge. The monkey which Sally had not seen since she became part of the Triangle was there again. He threw a biscuit at the dog who seized it and ran wildly out of sight. But there were no beautiful Chinese ladies wearing robes of silk.

"Never mind," said Kitty. "We'll see them in Chinatown! We'll go there on Saturday to make sure!"

When Saturday came they set off after dinner, walking steadily through the drab streets.

They searched and searched. They came across Chinese restaurants with wonderful and strange words like pictures painted on the windows. Sally hoped this would be like the Irish writing she had learned at school in Cork.

She looked again and shook her head.

"It isn't the same at all!" she said sorrowfully.

Kitty took them to a restaurant where they had steaming bowls of chicken noodle soup that cost a shilling each. To the younger ones this seemed terribly extravagant. But now and then, not often, it made Kitty happy to be extravagant.

They sat on high stools with their bowls of soup standing on a narrow shelf running the length of the window. Each had a slice of crisp toast. They sat there, breaking the toast into the soup and tasting delicious spoonfuls.

"Do the Chinese have this every day?" asked Sally, feeling warmer and more comfortable with every mouthful.

Kitty nodded.

"And rice and dumpling and chicken that melts in your mouth!"

"You'd have to be rich to do that every day," Sally warned her sister.

"When you and Dom are earning money we'll be rich enough to have everything we want."

The two younger ones looked at one another proudly, thinking how grand they would be.

On another expedition they went through a great tunnel under the Thames. When they went down into the darkness Sally shut her eyes dreading to see the water pouring down on them. It was a long tunnel with motors and buses rumbling through. By the time they had reached the other end she had decided that nothing would happen to them.

"But I'll never go down there again!" she told herself as she came out into the sunlight.

They saw huge blocks of flats like mountains with rows and rows of windows jutting into the sky. They passed a village of gay red-brick houses with gardens round them, designed and built as a memorial to a great man who once lived in East London.

"That's a lot better than an ugly old statue!" said Kitty approvingly.

Alongside a row of dark, desolate, one-storey houses which seemed to be sinking into the mud, they came to an opening where, on the opposite side of the river, they saw a dream-like ship with slender masts and spars standing out against the darkening sky as if drawn with the delicate pen of an artist.

"I wish I could go back to Cork in that!" cried Sally.

"That's the *Cutty Sark*!" Dominick announced, proud of his knowledge. "It was built years and years ago before there were steamships. Part of the year it carried wheat from foreign parts. When there wasn't any wheat it brought tea from China. It's a clipper, that's what it is!"

"It must be terribly old!" sighed Kitty. "But it's very lovely. I wish I could paint it!"

Cork was slipping out of Sally's mind—far,

far away, though she dreamed of looking at the grey-brown waters of the Thames and finding they had changed to the dancing sunlit waves of the Lee.

New impressions were crowding in. The Triangle was still strange and the inhabitants bewildering but full of interest, each with a different story.

Day by day Sally learned more about them. But it had not ceased to be an adventure to come through the narrow passage, climb the creaking stairs, hurry past shut or open doors and come out upon the top floor where masts and rigging and funnels were as close neighbours as slate roofs and chimney-pots.

She had given up trying to make Dominick regard her as a big sister. Not only was he two inches taller but he had a knowledge of London which made her ashamed of her own ignorance.

He knew the routes and destinations of every bus that swept by them on their way to school, for they still went out together, though they came back separately. He knew all the towns the long-distance buses and touring coaches passed through, the miles they travelled, their times of starting and returning.

Dominick was almost as knowledgeable about the boats on the river. He could plan voyages all over the world, draw maps to illustrate the journeys and estimate the cost.

"I'll never pay to go on a ship or a train," he told Sally one day on their way to school. "Not when I'm grown up!"

"If you want to travel, you'll have to," she protested, "unless you mean to be a stowaway!"

She gazed at him with startled eyes.

Dominick shook his head.

"Of course not! I mean to be a traveller, a commercial traveller. Not one of those chaps who lug big bundles of clothes or curtains into drapers' shops but a man who travels in—"

He paused, his mind ranging over the saleable goods of the world, smiled and flung up his head.

"I know, Sally! I'll travel in diamonds."

Sally drew a deep breath.

"Dom! You're wonderful! Where will you get them from?"

Dom frowned. He didn't know. He had heard one of the boys at school talking about an uncle who travelled in jewels and had at once considered this a sparkling career.

"How does a traveller in diamonds start?" Sally wanted to know.

Dominick hadn't an idea. His gay, confident expression faded. He looked very young and helpless.

"Never mind! You'll find out!" Sally told him. "By the time you're old enough to leave school, you'll know everything there is to know about diamonds. I'm sure you will!"

Dominick looked at her.

"Do you really think that? Honest?"

Sally looked very serious. She knew this was important.

"I do!" she answered. "You're brave and clever. If other people know all about diamonds, why shouldn't you?"

Dominick was cheerful again. He swung his school-bag round his head.

"I'll race you," he cried, darting forward.

Sally wasn't ready to run. She was thinking. Here was Dominick younger than herself, even if he were bigger, planning his future, while she was content to take one day at a time, content if she succeeded in avoiding trouble or pleasing her friends.

"One day when I wake I'll find myself grown up," she thought mournfully, "and I'll have done nothing about it."

"Hurry up, lazybones!" cried Dominick.

She began running and he waited for her.

"I'll be home late today," he told her as they stopped breathlessly and strolled along in the pale sunshine while heavy lorries thundered by on their way to the docks. All along the road buses stopped and started, stopped and started, with passengers crowding on and off. Sally glanced curiously at the destination boards.

Dominick read them out.

"Hampstead! That's where the heath is. We should go there on Bank Holiday. A boy told me he won a coconut at a shy there."

"What's a shy?" Sally wanted to know.

"Something to do with throwing balls," Dom told her.

"Look!" he went on. "Bromley, Greenwich—that's where the giant telescope is, in the Observatory. You can see what the moon is really like if you look through."

"Have you done it?" asked Sally.

"Not yet, but I will," he boasted. "Finsbury Park! Don't know that! Ah, there's Epping Forest! We should have a picnic there one day!"

"What is the forest like?" asked his sister.

Dom wasn't listening. The names of all the places he hadn't seen were passing through his mind like music.

"Are you playing hurling after school?" she asked.

He shook his head.

"Not this evening. We are learning Irish at

the Club. You should come."

"I will when I've an evening to spare," Sally promised.

"What are you doing tonight that's so awfully special?"

"You know I've been staying in school for cookery lessons?"

Dominick grinned but did not speak.

"Well, today I'm going to rush straight home, and when you and Kitty come in there'll be a big hot jam tart in the oven all ready to eat!"

"Mm! Mm!" said the boy, smacking his lips. "If I'm late you'll save me my share, won't you?"

"Of course I will! And Kitty would if I forgot!"

"What sort of jam?" Dominick wanted to know. "I like blackcurrant best."

Sally sighed.

"So do I! Only Kitty hasn't opened the new jar yet. I thought I'd clear out all the old jars and have them clean and ready for the man to collect. A mixed jam tart should taste very nice."

"Scrumptious!" agreed Dom. "Well, goodbye, Sally! Don't forget, make a real big one!"

He dashed off to join a crowd of boys, for the school bell was ringing.

Sally ran too. But she had farther to go and the porter was just closing the gates as she reached them.

"Nearly late again," he growled. But he let her through.

When Sally got inside, to her amazement and delight she saw her own name in the list of the six best girls for the week. She saw Marcella's name too, but Marcella was used to success while Sally had never been in the top six before.

"Won't Kitty be pleased when I tell her," she thought. "I'll have to make that tart really good to celebrate. Next time she won't mind which jam I use."

Marcella's mother had been making ginger biscuits and Marcella brought two bags, one for herself and one for Sally. They sat munching the biscuits at lunch time when they had finished their packets of sandwiches and were drinking hot cocoa. Sally felt very happy.

"It must be lovely to have a mother," she said.

Marcella looked at her friend in sympathy.

"Poor Sally! I forgot, and you haven't a father either. I couldn't bear that."

"I have a father!" cried Sally indignantly. "He went away to America before my mother died. But he'll be coming back—one day!"

"Will he be rich?" asked Marcella. "Oh, Sally, won't it be lovely if he does come back with heaps of money!"

Suddenly she frowned and gazed at her friend with real concern.

"Sally! Did you leave your London address with someone in Cork? Someone where you lived before you came to London?"

Sally shook her head.

"You should have!" cried Marcella. "Suppose he goes looking for you and finds you gone and no one can tell him where you are. Oh, Sally, you are a goose! I wonder now, did Kitty think of it before she brought you away!"

"I'm sure she didn't," said Sally sorrowfully. "We were in such a hurry and in a muddle too, for when she and Dom came to Cork they had to go back at once, the moment they found me. The ship wouldn't wait. And the people I was with were just setting off for the United States. What will my father do if he comes back and there isn't a trace of us?"

Marcella sat thinking hard.

"I know!" she said at last. "I'll tell my father. He'll know what you should do. He always knows what to do. That's because he's a doctor. Come along, the school bell's just stopped ringing."

Marcella was so confident that her father could settle any difficulty in the world that Sally ceased worrying about this problem. She felt far more concerned over the jam tart she had determined to make. She wanted it to be something very special.

That morning it had seemed easy. Already she could see it in her imagination—light, hot and fragrant. There was an appetizing odour of well-baked pastry and hot jam. Kitty and Dom would tell her how good it was. But when she mounted the stairs on her return from school, put her key in the door, turned it and found herself alone, she began to feel a little uneasy.

Pulling off her coat and hat she remembered to hang them on the door of her own little room. Next she opened the cupboard where Kitty kept flour, salt, sugar, bread soda, tea, cocoa, jam—everything belonging to this department.

The butter, margarine and dripping were on the little window-sill with a wire screen over them. The pastry-board, roller and a small enamel bowl for mixing were on the top shelf of the cupboard.

This cupboard was so neat Sally doubted if she had a right to disarrange it. Kitty was always cleaning and rearranging the little flat and Sally was proud to help her. Yet she knew that her help often only gave her sister more work.

"This time I'll be so careful Kitty will really

be pleased with me," she told herself.

She took out the paper bag of flour and opened it. A white cloud rose in the air and settled on Sally's hair and frock. The table looked as if there had been a light fall of snow.

Sally frowned.

"Perhaps I should be more careful but who'd think a tiny scatter of flour could spread so far!" she exclaimed.

Reading the instructions printed on the bag she nodded wisely.

"It's self-raising flour, so it can't help rising up and falling over everything. Kitty will understand!"

She continued reading out loud.

" 'Add four beaten-up eggs and a little salt to one pound of flour, mix into a stiff batter with milk.'

"That's pancakes!" she said.

" 'Rub four ounces of butter or three ounces of beef dripping into half a pound of flour, add four ounces of sugar and a little salt, flavour with ginger, coconut or vanilla, put into greased basin or tin.

" 'Add six ounces finely chopped suet and a little salt to one pound of flour, mix into a light dough with water, turn into cloth, boil for two and a half hours.' "

The print was small and the bag was crumpled. Sally could not see what the recipes were intended for.

"That's not the way to make a jam tart!" she muttered resentfully. "It can't be!"

The more she read the more confused she became. How she wished pretty Miss Lewis—the cookery teacher—was there, her eyes laughing, her fair curly hair speckled with flour, her slim fingers caked with dough.

The cookery class was always in a muddle. Yet on the stroke of the hour the food in the saucepan or oven was cooked, the table clean and the girls in the class busy washing their hands, while the girl whose turn it was to take home whatever had been cooked looked happy and proud.

It had never come to Sally's turn so far.

"I'll show what I can do at home, all by myself," she said, and continued reading out loud.

" 'Two breakfast cupfuls self-raising flour, one large spoonful of sugar, one egg (well beaten), a spoonful of spice, a pinch of salt, half a cupful of currants, well washed in cold water and dried in a clean cloth, half a cupful of sultanas, a quarter of a pound of mixed peel, cut finely. Mix well, stir in sufficient milk and water to form a stiff dough.' "

How much easier was cooking when the directions were read out very, very slowly by Miss Lewis, as she walked round the table, never interfering but ready to help with mixing or advice.

Sally rubbed her nose uncertainly, with a floury hand.

"This isn't for jam tart pastry!" she exclaimed. "I'm reading the wrong directions. Here is my one—the third down. I'll do it, a bit at a time!

"I mustn't get flummoxed. Mrs Mooney said I always did. But I won't this time. I can't measure everything. I'd never have the tart ready. I must guess at some!"

She poured out half the flour in the bag into the mixing-bowl, tipped out all the sugar left in the sugar-basin, mixed them well and let water trickle in from the tap. She stirred and stirred.

"It's a bit thin. Maybe it won't matter," she thought, trying to remember Miss Lewis's instructions and wishing she had watched her sister when she made an apple-tart.

"I can't expect to be as good as Kitty straight off!" she told herself. "If only my tart looks proper I won't mind too much, even if it does taste a bit queer.

"Dom eats so quickly he'll swallow it before he has a chance to notice and Kitty is too kind to say anything. She'll just be pleased I tried. Now, where's the tin?"

Sally found the tin, ready to be used, on the little dresser.

"I'm sure this should be greased so that the tart won't stick," she murmured, looking round for the butter.

"I know! It's on the window-sill!" she remembered.

As she opened the window and lifted the wire screen a terrible thought came to her.

Shouldn't she have mixed the flour with butter or dripping? Wasn't that the difference between a mixture for a cake and the one for pastry? No! Both had to be mixed with butter or dripping.

She was convinced of that. Or was she?

When Miss Lewis taught them to make a sponge-cake, she had mixed flour, eggs and sugar together. The only grease she used was the dripping Marcella rubbed on the tin.

"I wish Marcella was here. She remembers everything! Or nearly everything!" reflected Sally.

Then she smiled.

"I know. I'll put a thick layer of dripping on

the bottom of the tin. When it gets hot it will mix itself up with the dough. No one will be able to tell I didn't mix it in first. When it gets a bit baked I'll spread the jam over it. That will cover everything!"

Sally poured the mixture into the tin. A thick layer stuck to the bottom of the mixing-bowl, for she hadn't stirred quite as well as she should.

"Bother!" she cried. "I can't let that lumpy bit go in with the rest. I know what I'll do! I'll make dollies with it, the way Mrs Mooney used to—one for Kitty, one for Dom and one for me!"

She made a nest of flour on the board and scraped every bit of dough from the bowl. With the tips of her fingers she worked it with the dry flour until it was quite stiff. Then she divided it into three.

"What shall I make?" she puzzled. "Dolls, babies, cats, dogs, horses? No! I'll make leprechauns for luck!"

Sally was happy again.

She pressed and moulded the small heaps of dough until three little bearded men, each complete with hammer, shoe and crock, lay on the board.

Sally greased another tin, laid the figures on it, side by side, lit the gas in the oven, slipped in the two tins and closed the oven door.

"Won't Kitty be pleased!" she thought triumphantly.

A smell of baking filled the room. Slowly Sally put back the empty sugar-basin, the dripping. She filled a kettle with water and, when it was hot, washed the mixing-bowl, the knives and spoon.

Then she remembered the jam.

There were four jam jars in a corner of the top shelf in the cupboard, each containing a little jam. Sally took out the tin in which the pastry was beginning to brown and scraped every bit of jam from the jars. It made a thick layer and the rich, tempting odour made her sniff with hungry anticipation.

"At last I'm doing something worth while," she said, talking out loud for company's sake. "Maybe I'll soon be able to do all the cooking and Kitty will have more time for reading and visiting her friends. And she'll be able to do more painting."

Sally leaned from the big wide window and looked out at the huddle of barges and steam boats. They were all strange craft and she sighed regretfully over the absence of the little monkey who used to sit up, watching her and catching crusts or sweets she threw out to him.

"I'd like a monkey of my own," she decided.

"Maybe Dom would like a dog better, and I know Kitty would love one. Only we couldn't leave a dog by himself all day. Now, why couldn't we have a kitten? That might be the best of all!"

She had dropped some crumbs on the narrow stretch of waste land below. A few venturesome sparrows settled there and were busy scratching and squabbling over their finds. One flew up and perched on a neighbouring window-sill. It looked at her with bright inquisitive eyes, its tiny head cocked sideways.

Sally took a biscuit from the dresser, and breaking this in small pieces, she tossed a scrap to the sparrow. The tiny bird flew up and caught it neatly.

Gradually the sparrow came nearer, then it fluttered back.

"One day I'll have them all coming to this window-sill," said Sally proudly. "Next time I bake a tart I'll make a lot of little birds too. They'd look grand! Only it would be a pity to eat them."

She had no more crumbs and the sparrow flew away to the others below.

"I can't have a kitten," said Sally. "It would frighten the birds away!"

She drew back from the window and frowned.

"What a dreadful smell!" she cried out in horror, running to the oven and flinging open the door.

A cloud of smoke swirled out. Gasping she stooped down and turned off the gas.

"My lovely tart!" she lamented. "It's ruined! Oh, what will Kitty say?"

As if in answer Sally heard a key turning in the lock of the outer door and there was Kitty, her eyes anxious, staring at her sister in dismay.

"What's happened?" asked Kitty. "What an awful smell? What is burning?"

"I made a jam tart for tea and I forgot to turn off the gas when it was done. I didn't know it was cooked!"

To her surprise Kitty laughed.

"Cooked!" she echoed. "It's certainly well cooked!"

"I am sorry!" Sally stammered. "I wanted it to be a surprise!"

There were tears in her eyes and she looked so forlorn that Kitty stopped laughing at once.

"It's a shame!" she said kindly. "But don't be so upset. Everyone makes mistakes to begin with. That's how we learn. Next time you'll make a wonderful jam tart, you see!"

Sally shook her head.

"I'll never try again!"

"That's cowardly!" declared Kitty. "You'll get nowhere if you let yourself be beaten by the first set-back. If you only knew the mistakes I've made, the stews I've burned, the cakes and tarts I've spoiled by forgetting something."

Sally nodded ruefully.

"I did forget to put any butter or dripping in," she confessed. "Pastry does need something like that, doesn't it?"

"It does!" agreed Kitty solemnly. "But cheer up now. I'll make a big thick raisin cake cooked on the pan. You can help me with it, that's the best way to learn!"

She closed the oven door and set the window open wide so that by the time Dominick came charging up the stairs there was only the smell of the raisin cake and the steam from the boiling kettle.

"This is a scrumptious cake," mumbled Dominick with his mouth full, when they sat down to tea. "I was starving! Only didn't you say you were going to make a jam tart?" he demanded, leaning across the table to gaze sternly at Sally.

Kitty answered for her.

"Sally will make a jam tart another time. She's learning that at school. I'm the only one who can teach her to make this kind of cake. So there you are. Another piece?"

"You bet!" said Dominick.

15
There's a Stranger Asking Questions!

hen she woke the next morning Sally hadn't a notion that anything special was going to happen. She remembered how kind Kitty had been when she spoilt the jam tart and resolved that in the future she would do everything properly and avoid disaster.

"I'll clean the tins and the oven for a start!" she decided.

She heard Kitty calling.

"Breakfast's ready, sleepy-head! You'll have to wash later!"

Sally jumped out of bed, pulled on her clothes and rushed to the big room.

"I didn't know it was time. I was thinking. Why didn't you call me?" she asked reproachfully.

"I did call you and here you are!" retorted Kitty. "Make yourself clean and tidy before you go out. Have you your key? Have you Dom? I'm off now. I've cut your sandwiches. Goodbye and be as good as you can!"

"Goodbye, Kitty, goodbye!" chorused Sally and Dominick.

Sally ate two slices of bread and butter as well as a big red apple. She drank two cups of tea.

"There's plenty more," she told Dominick. "Want some?"

"Not me!" he answered. "Hurry yourself! I'm doing the washing-up this morning. It's my turn!"

"You'd better let me do it," said Sally. "You see yesterday I did try to make a jam tart and it turned out a horrid mess. I made some little figures of dough too but I didn't dare look at them!"

She knelt down before the gas oven and Dominick watched with an amused grin.

Opening the door she peeped in timidly, gasped and sat back on her heels, looking very puzzled.

The big tin which had held the tart and the small one with the three leprechaun figures were clean, shining and quite empty.

"I must have dreamed it all!" thought Sally.

She looked back at Dominick and understood.

No! It wasn't a dream! It had really happened. But Kitty had cleared away all signs of her blunder.

"Isn't Kitty a darling!" she murmured. "The tart doesn't matter now. But I'm sorry about the leprechauns. You know, Dom, they were so real I wouldn't have liked to eat them."

Dominick filled the kettle and gathered the breakfast dishes in a big enamel bowl. He was unusually silent and Sally wondered if he had a toothache or was in trouble at school. She wiped and he washed and they went off together without saying a word until they had left the Triangle behind and were waiting at the big crossing.

They stood outside a big shop with wide windows. Men were carrying in crates of delph. Sally, staring after them, saw that the windows were filled with little pottery groups of children and animals. There were rows of them. Some were just ornaments, others were religious statuettes. She frowned as she studied them.

"I wonder how they were made," she said aloud. "My leprechauns were better!"

"Come on now!" said Dominick impatiently,

giving her arm a tug. "We can cross!"

She followed her brother. He had to take her hand and pull her with him, for she did not see the traffic or the hurrying crowds. She was feeling again that thrill in her finger-tips that she had when she moulded the leprechauns out of dough.

As they drew near the school Dom glanced thoughtfully at this sister smaller yet older than himself. He knew she wasn't very clever at lessons. But Sister Agnes had told Kitty that one day they would all be proud of her.

Dominick thought the burnt jam tart was a joke and he would never have bothered about the leprechauns only that Kitty had been so excited when she found them in the oven.

"How lucky they are not really burnt, only baked hard so that they look like brown clay," she had told him. "I'll show them to Mrs Mercer. She'll forget my poor little pictures when she sees these. I always knew Sally had something in her!"

Dominick remembered Kitty's words as he left Sally at the school gate.

"Kitty wants us to come straight home," he said. "I'll meet you here after school."

Sally nodded as she darted inside the gates and ran to catch up with Marcella who was disappearing between the big double doors.

"I hope she remembers," thought Dominick. "I'll get back here as soon as I can."

One thing Sally liked about this school was that children came there from all over the world. That morning she sat with a small Chinese girl and an older girl from India. Kitty had told her how lucky she was to know children from different countries while she was so young.

"They never talk," Sally had complained. "I want to hear about the places they come from and then I could tell them about Wise's Hill."

"I expect they're homesick," Kitty told her. "When I first came over I think I'd have died of loneliness only I had to earn my living and then take care of Dom. I used to dream about you and wonder what was happening, though I trusted the Mooneys. They were kind to you, weren't they?"

"They were indeed!" answered Sally. "Do tell me, Kitty, how old were you and where did you and Dom live when you first came? You didn't come to the Triangle at first, did you?"

"No!" said Kitty. "Not at first. I was sixteen. You were eight and Dom was only six. A girl I knew was coming over and didn't want to come alone. She had found work in a factory and said there was a place for me too. The Mooneys thought it was a great chance.

"They promised to look after you and Dom till I could send for you. When mother died she left us a little money and everyone expected daddy would come back from America. But he didn't come. The money was nearly all gone when I crossed to London.

"I hated working in the factory. One day I was wandering in a strange part of London. I stopped to look at a shop. The window was filled with brooches and necklaces, old pictures without frames, wine-glasses with gold rims, china ornaments and, right in the middle, a picture of an Irish mountain with little thatched whitewashed cabins along the road. It was this that made me stop!

"Then, underneath the picture, I saw a notice written on a piece of paper, '*Wanted, Young Assistant. Apply Within.*' "

Kitty had paused.

Sally sat waiting in silence.

"I went inside," continued Kitty very slowly. "I met Mrs Mercer and everything in London was changed. It was through her I came to the Triangle and had Dom with me; through her I brought you over; through her I can send you and Dom to such a good school."

Sally had listened to Kitty telling the story of her London adventures so that she had only to sit still and close her eyes and she could hear it all again. She was doing this now as she sat in school.

Suddenly she woke to her surroundings. The Indian girl touched Sally's hand with her long, slim, brown fingers.

"You are dreaming," she said in a soft voice. "Are you homesick too?"

"I have no home in Ireland," murmured Sally, "only the one my sister has made for us here. Have you a sister?"

"No talking in class," said Miss O'Grady. But she smiled.

"Poor little exiles," she thought. "I'm glad they're making friends."

The Chinese girl had been listening. She did not understand all she heard. Yet she had a feeling of kinship with these two. They had not noticed how often and how deliberately the young teacher had put them together. But she did, for she was lonelier.

"Miss O'Grady tries to make life better for us," she thought gravely, looking from face to face.

Marcella, who wanted to be with Sally, noticed it too.

"Why do they try to arrange our friendships?" she thought resentfully. "All the Irish should go together and all the foreigners keep to themselves."

She frowned at the three girls sitting in front of her, their heads close together. Then she saw that Miss O'Grady was watching too and felt ashamed.

"I should be glad, only Sally is my friend. I know how clever she is!"

She was with Sally when they came out from school.

"I'm going to have a birthday party," she announced. "My mother says I can ask who I like. You're the first I've asked!"

Sally was delighted.

"Oh, Marcella, how lovely!" she cried. "Who else will you ask?"

Marcella's eyes roved over the noisy chattering throng of girls. She hadn't many real friends, for until the last few months she had been away at boarding school. Yet her mother would expect her to have more than one guest.

Sally saw the Indian girl, tall, grave, courteous, drawing back to let a laughing group pass before her. Near her was the Chinese girl and, on the step below, was Florrie Cox, a small dark girl, her brown face shining. Sally had taken an immediate liking to her.

Sally breathed deeply, frowned and grasped Marcella's hand.

"Would you do something very special for me?" she asked.

Marcella smiled at Sally's serious face.

"Of course I would," she said.

"Ask Florrie Cox to the party!" Sally blurted out.

The dark, thin, little girl's quick ears caught her name. Sally saw the flash of her big expressive eyes, her white teeth and tossing hair. There she was beside them.

"You call me?" she inquired, glancing from one to the other.

Marcella looked at her gravely.

"I'm having a birthday party next Wednesday. My mother and I will be delighted if you will come and, of course, your brother too."

Sally closed her eyes. She was thrilled, for every girl in the school knew that Florrie's brother was a musical prodigy.

It began one day when Florrie was at the piano stumbling through a five-finger exercise. The solemn, stocky little boy pushed her from the stool and played quickly, without one mistake, every exercise in the book. He was only six, he couldn't read, but every piece of music he heard once he was able to play accurately.

Florrie was very excited and proud. Her mother, a golden-haired, blue-eyed young widow from Yarmouth, did not know whether to be delighted or sorry.

"I always hoped Johnnie would get a position in a shop or an office one day," she said. "But maybe he'd be happier teaching children to play the piano. After all, his father was a teacher."

Florrie had coaxed Sister Agnes to hear her little brother play.

The nun's eyes sparkled.

"Your brother has a gift!" she declared. "It must not be wasted."

Florrie thankfully gave up her seat at the piano to him. Up till then he was a lazy boy but now he rose early to practise scales.

"You will come?" asked Marcella again, for Florrie had remained silent.

Sally opened her eyes wide in amazement. Surely the dark girl would not refuse. Suddenly she realized that Florrie couldn't speak. There were tears in her eyes and her lips were trembling. Always at school she had felt she was a stranger. Until her brother's talent had been discovered she had been afraid of a world that could become suddenly hostile for no reason at all.

Marcella tried to imitate her mother's grown-up manner.

"It will give us great pleasure if you will come," she said.

"Thank you—very—very much!" Florrie stammered at last.

Marcella saw that Sally's two friends, the Indian and the Chinese girl, were waiting for a chance to say goodbye to Sally before they went home.

She made up her mind quickly and went straight over to them.

"I'm having a birthday party next week," she said. "And I want it to be an international party. Sally Nolan is coming. She is Irish, like me. I'm asking two London friends. Florrie Cox is coming and so is her brother. I want you both to come, will you?"

The Chinese girl bowed, and smiled her agreement.

"I must ask my father's permission," said the Indian girl. "But I am sure he will be very pleased."

Marcella turned to Sally.

"We must have some boys," she said. "There will be my two brothers and Johnnie Cox. Do you think your brother will come?"

"I'm sure he would," Sally told her. "He can

sing and say poetry too! He isn't a bit shy."

"Boys never are!" said Marcella. "I'd like your sister to come, only I suppose she's too old."

Sally ran through the gates and there was Dominick, waiting and wondering where she had got to.

"Dom!" cried Sally. "We're invited to a party!"

"What kind? Where? Who's asking us?" he demanded.

"It's Marcella! She's giving an international party."

Dominick's eyes opened so wide it was a wonder they didn't fall out.

"What kind of a party is that?" he asked.

"People from different countries. There's an Indian and a Chinese girl. Then there's Florrie Cox and her brother Johnnie."

"Any boys?" he asked suspiciously.

"Didn't you hear? There's Johnnie Cox!"

"A kid!" said Dominick scornfully "He can't be more than seven!"

"Marcella has two brothers, both older than she is," announced Sally.

"I'll come!" decided Dominick. "I like Marcella! Now I'll race you home."

Sally opened her mouth to ask why he was in such a hurry but he was running along the street, choosing the wide kerb where the passage was clear. So she ran too, keeping close behind.

"Hi!" he called suddenly. "Hi! Stop, Kitty Nolan!"

There was Kitty just going into the Triangle. She looked over her shoulder, smiled and waited.

"Had a good day?" she asked.

"Never mind our day!" Dominick answered impatiently. "What's your news?"

"Wait until we're upstairs!" she told him. "We don't want a public meeting!"

She put her key in the lock, went along the hall and began to climb the stairs. A door above opened and old Mrs Dillon peered out at them.

She beckoned Kitty to come close. The others paused on the stairs and waited curiously.

"Listen to me, Kitty Nolan," the old woman whispered. "There's been a stranger round the courtyard asking questions."

"Questions?" repeated Kitty. "What about?"

"Tisn't what, love!" the old woman told her. "Tis who! Now who would be wanting to know where ye came from, how many there are of ye and the like of that? Do ye know anyone that had a right to know?"

Kitty shook her head.

"Yet there's a stranger going round asking

questions and giving no raysons!"

"What did you tell him?" Kitty asked.

The old woman folded her arms, gripping both elbows in her thin small hands so that the knuckles showed white against her black shawl.

"Sure, child, I never set eyes on the chap, let alone had any old chat wid him. Twas at the Stores yonder. They're used to questions there and, like decent people everywhere, they give no answers about other folks' concerns. I'm just telling ye what was told to me!"

"Thank you very much, Mrs Dillon," said Kitty as the old bent woman backed into her room and shut the door.

Kitty looked serious and troubled. Sally wondered if she would tell Dominick and herself what she feared, but by the time they reached the door of their little fortress Kitty was smiling again.

When the door was closed she turned to Dom.

"Can you guess what's happened?" she asked.

"Something good?" he questioned.

"Very good! Guess what!"

The boy shook his head. His eyes rested on Sally. Suddenly she felt excited. Something thrilling had happened and it concerned her.

She was sure of that.

"Do tell us, Kitty!" she pleaded. "Please do!"

Kitty leaned back against the table.

"You remember those three little leprechauns you made out of dough?" she asked her sister.

Sally felt ashamed.

"I made an awful muddle with my cooking," she confessed. "I'll do better next time. It was good of you to clean up the mess. I meant to do that!"

"You are a little goose," said Kitty affectionately. "I know the tart was burnt. That can happen to anyone! Next time you'll remember to look at the oven. But it's your three leprechauns that mattered. They were baked hard so that they looked as if they were carved in wood.

"I took them to show Mrs Mercer. She was delighted and put them in the window. She sold all three and has sent you seven and sixpence, that is two and sixpence each for them.

"She wants you to make her a dozen, using clay or plaster, and she will give you five shillings each for them. She says you can keep on making them because they'll sell for ever!"

Sally stared open-mouthed. She could not speak. Then she drew a deep breath.

"It's wonderful!" she declared. "And I felt so

miserable about my burnt jam tart!"

Kitty laughed.

"Let's have tea! To celebrate your success, Sally, I've been extravagant. We have a veal-and-ham pie, three custard tarts, three bags of crisps and a bunch of grapes. We're going to celebrate!"

"We should have wine!" said Dominick reproachfully. "You can't celebrate without wine!"

"We'll make do with tea!" his sister told him gaily.

Sally turned to the window. Years seemed to have passed since she had first looked out on masts and funnels rising against the London sky. If only this could have happened in Cork! Yet even there she remembered she had been lonely.

"Now I'm not lonely any more!" she said aloud.

Kitty put her arm around her young sister.

The door swung open abruptly and in dashed Dominick, out of breath, holding a big bottle of cider.

"I got this at the corner shop," he said. "Now we can drink to Sally's success properly. And, Kitty! I saw the man who has been round asking about us.

"He was talking to old Jerry Flynn. They were going along the Mile End Road. He's the man who was at the picture gallery and the hurling match. No one else could be asking questions about us!"

Kitty nodded.

"I expect you're right!" she said.

But soon they were all too busy celebrating Sally's success to bother about anything else.

16
Shape and Colour

hey ate every crumb of the veal-and-ham pie, emptied out the three bags of crisps, nibbled idly at the custard tarts and left the two bunches of grapes, one green, one black, untouched. The bottle of cider was still half full when Kitty put it in the cupboard.

"Won't it stop fizzing?" asked Dominick anxiously.

"What does that matter?" Kitty wanted to know. "It's good cider and no one would expect us to drink it all at once!"

She put the kettle on the gas stove.

"If that's for washing up," said Dominick, "I'll do it!"

"You're a treasure!" his sister told him. "But it's for tea. I need two strong cups. Now I've discovered Sally's going to be a credit to us, I

they looked wonderful. Mrs Mercer wants more. Only I think she'd like clay or maybe wood."

"I don't want to make wooden leprechauns," muttered Sally. "Though I'd sooner do that than make them out of stone."

"Don't worry! There's always a way of doing what you want, if you're clever," Kitty consoled her. "We'll go to the Club on Saturday night, there's bound to be someone there who'll know."

On Friday evening Kitty came home with a big bundle of fried fish and chips in her green string bag. Dominick hadn't arrived but Sally had laid the table and the kettle was boiling.

Kitty put the fish and chips in the oven to get hot, took off her coat and washed her hands. Her eyes were so bright and her cheeks so flushed Sally guessed something important had happened.

She waited a little apprehensively.

"I hope I don't have to start banging on old stones with a hammer," she thought.

At last Kitty turned to her.

"Guess what I'm going to tell you!"

Sally shook her head.

"I'm not very good at guessing."

Kitty laughed.

"You are an exasperating young monkey! I'm

the one that's excited, not you. That's not natural!"

"I don't know what you're excited about," Sally pointed out. "If you tell me, maybe I'll be excited too!"

"Maybe you will and maybe you won't," sighed Kitty. "Still, as you're so cool, the news can wait till Dom comes in. He'll be excited, even if you're not."

"It won't interfere with Marcella's birthday party, will it?" asked Sally anxiously.

Kitty was combing her hair at the mirror hanging beside the window. She glanced over her shoulder.

"You'll forget all about Marcella's party when you hear my news," she declared. "Marcella isn't the whole of the world!"

Sally looked startled. She had never before heard that note of sharpness in her sister's voice.

"Kitty! Would you like to go to the party? Mrs Lanigan wanted you to be asked but Marcella didn't like to ask you because it's her fourteenth birthday and she thought you'd feel too old!"

"Her two brothers will be there, won't they?" asked Kitty.

Sally nodded.

"And how old are they?"

"The youngest is sixteen, the other is eighteen. Of course he isn't at school, he's at college. The Sharans are coming too and one of them is a really big boy."

"And how old do you think I am?" asked Kitty.

She was smiling again.

"Kitty is pretty, very pretty!" thought Sally, feeling she was seeing her sister for the first time. "But how old is she?"

"I don't know," she confessed. "Of course you're grown up!"

Kitty laughed.

"I'm nineteen!" she announced. "Is that very old? Am I too old for Marcella's party?"

"I'll tell Marcella you'll come! She'll be delighted!" said Sally.

"Here's Dom!" cried Kitty as the door was flung open and he came quickly into the room. He looked expectantly at Sally.

"I haven't broken the news to her yet," Kitty told him. "I've been trying to rouse her curiosity. She hasn't any! Listen, Sally! Mrs Mercer says you must study art. She's going to find out if you're too young to go to an art school. I'm to bring you to the shop tomorrow. She wants to talk to you and to see what you're like."

Sally blinked.

"You mean—I'm to learn how to make figures properly?"

Kitty nodded. But even now she wasn't sure. Mrs Mercer had been excited over Sally's leprechauns but was there a future for Sally in such work? She wanted Sally and Dom to have a better life than she had. She looked at Dom.

"Mrs Mercer will know," he declared. "We can all go and talk to her. Sally'd like me to back her up and I want to see the shop."

Kitty sighed but it was a sigh of relief. Dom was so sensible, though he was only a boy and a young one at that. She was still a little afraid of Mrs Mercer who, for all her kindness, would sometimes fly into a temper over nothing at all. She hoped Dom as well as Sally would make an impression on the curio dealer.

They ate their tea almost in silence.

Dom was trying to decide whether he would stick to hurling only, or to football, or would it be possible to combine both. He thought how lucky Kitty was to be able to earn a living at what she liked best.

"She's only just started," he told himself. "All the famous artists are as old as the hills. Kitty may be famous one day!"

"I'll wash up," said Kitty. "You two polish your shoes and see your best clothes are ready for tomorrow. We'll have to rush off the minute we've had our dinners. I'll be home as early as I can."

***

It seemed that Saturday was on them almost before they'd finished with Friday.

"I'm lucky to have Saturday afternoon off," said Kitty as she tucked the hand-knitted green muffler inside her coat. "Mrs Mercer stays in the shop all day. She likes it better than anywhere else."

She snatched up her little brown handbag and they could hear her running downstairs.

"Lucky the staircase is a twisty one," chuckled Dominick. "Kitty would give one jump and land at the bottom if she could! More tea, Sally!"

They hurried over their preparations and were out in the Triangle as early as if they were going to school, for they had to do the week-end shopping while Kitty went to work.

Sally kept close to Dominick. She was sure she could never be so clever as he was at picking out the crispest celery, the sweetest apples, the firmest tomatoes, and he was so proud of his skill in bargaining he had no wish to hand over the task to anyone.

Kitty had left vegetable stew on the gas stove

with the tap turned very low, and when they returned the mixed savoury smells of onions and herbs made them realize that the frosty air as well as their haste had made them ravenous.

Sally stirred the stew while Dominick changed into his best suit. Then she put on her best clothes. They were both looking hungrily at the simmering saucepan when they heard their sister's light step coming up the stairs.

Dominick opened the door with a flourish and bowed her in.

"Everything's ready, Kitty," he declared. "We're waiting and starving!"

Kitty looked at their smiling eager faces and neat clothes with pleasure. She was proud of earning her living and keeping a home for the others. Now she felt that the future was opening the door on what might be a real chance for Sally. So she felt happy.

She looked at the table—the clean white cloth, the gleaming knives, forks and spoons, the flowers in the centre. She sniffed the soup with appreciation and laid a paper bag on the table.

"The first mince-pies of the year," she declared. "We still have to celebrate!"

They were all excited, happy, laughing.

"What are we celebrating now?" Sally asked

herself. "Perhaps it's because it's Saturday. Saturday is a lovely day!"

She gazed out of the window. For the first time there were no masts, no funnels to be seen. A few sparrows, perched on a low roof, gazed uncertainly at a strutting seagull across the tiny bridge.

"What a lovely bird," thought Sally. "Only its beak is cruel, so are its hard eyes. No! They're not cruel. They're wanting to know. Wish I could make a seagull!"

She felt Kitty and Dominick looking at her.

"Mrs Mercer says that Sally must have clay to work in," said Kitty. "She's not sure where we should get it but she'll find out."

"Can we go now?" asked Sally urgently, terrified lest this amazing woman who knew so much would be gone before they reached the shop.

"A cup of tea first!" said Kitty firmly.

"And a mince-pie!" added Dominick. "Now remember, Sally! Wish while you're eating yours. It's the first mince-pie of the year, so that wish will come true."

Sally sipped her tea.

"How empty it looks out there," she murmured. "Only that lovely seagull and the silly little sparrows."

"I thought Cork would be empty," said Kitty. "I'd heard so much of people going away and never coming back. Yet when we went to bring you here, there were crowds of the nicest, friendliest people in the world."

At last they closed the door of the flat and went sedately downstairs. Old Mrs Dillon looked out at them.

"Is anything wrong?" she asked, gazing anxiously at the three grouped together in a dark corner of the stairs. "Sure, ye're not sending the young one back? Don't slip away one by one. When ye go, go together!"

"We will, Mrs Dillon," promised Kitty. "We're not leaving the Triangle yet. We're going to see someone who may give Sally a chance to be rich and famous!"

The old woman clasped her hands.

"God be praised!" she cried. "Will something fine and good come out of this desolate place at last. I knew the first time I set eyes on Sally she had something different in her. Off wid ye! If there's good coming to ye, thanks be! But if ye're disappointed, remember the young always have the future. Away! And may good luck go wid ye!"

"Goodbye and thank you!" said Sally.

Her voice was hoarse. Now she was excited.

She didn't know what it all meant, except that if she pleased Mrs Mercer, she might be able to do what she wanted.

Sally frowned. If only she understood what that was. It was not at all clear to her.

They climbed on to a bus. Of course they went up on top and were lucky enough to find the front seats empty.

Until Sally came to London she had never been on a double-decker bus. The people in the Triangle were poor but not as poor as Sally's friends on Wise's Hill. Some living at the top and a few at the bottom, near the quays, had motor-cars of their own. But for most of the children a trip down the Lee in Cork was a luxury.

Sally, perched on the front seat of the swaying, jerking bus, speeding through the drab streets, leaving behind the life of docks and river, was far more thrilled than Kitty or Dominick.

When they came to Oxford Street, the grand shops seemed like a row of palaces. At the entrance of one a group of men were raising big Christmas-trees and fixing them on a ledge half-way up the great building.

Men and women were busy arranging the windows for the Christmas display. The dolls were so lifelike that Sally almost thought they must be alive. She gave a sudden, sideways glance at her brother and sister. They looked pleased at the sight but they hadn't that feeling of delight and wonder that she felt, looking at this for the first time. She caught a glimpse of a toy, mechanical circus in one window where clowns, monkeys, horses, lions and bears were doing amazing tricks.

"They're just toys!" Sally reminded herself.

She tried to be scornful. But how she envied the lucky people who handled dolls that could open and close their eyes, whose limbs were jointed so that they could sit bolt upright, stand or kneel.

"Of course I'm too big for dolls and toys now," she thought proudly.

As they stepped off the bus she stopped to stare at a boy running with a bundle of papers under his arm.

Her fingers itched. She longed for a lump of clay so that she could mould what she saw.

Kitty and Dominick waited.

Dominick laughed.

"Poor Sally! Look at her now! I bet if she had a lump of dough someone wanted to make a pudding with, she'd make a running boy for them!"

"How could she?" asked Kitty. "A statue is always still!"

Dominick made a face.

"Maybe it is! But do you know what Mr Reynolds told us in class? He said that an artist's ability to create a sense of motion is one of his greatest qualities."

"What else did he say?" asked Kitty.

Dominick didn't hear her. He was looking at Sally coming through the crowd as if she were in a dream.

Sally was no longer gazing at the wonderful shop windows where men were arranging circuses with toy clowns or marvellous farmyards with perfect animals: she was watching a boy running, as he would run for ever, in her mind.

Sally had forgotten why they were there. When the three of them turned into a lively street market with a narrow passage way between the stalls, where people pushed and jostled, she was surprised at the loveliness of the fruit and vegetables.

Lagging behind, she luxuriated in the shapes of the strange fruits displayed in the Soho market. Looking at a heap of red and green peppers she understood Kitty's love of colour that she put into her pictures.

"But shape matters more!" she decided firmly.

Dominick had to retrace his steps through the crowd in search of Sally and found her standing motionless in front of an old man who was making small animals out of sticks of coloured plasticine.

"How clever he is!" she murmured as she allowed Dominick to pull her away.

"We must hurry!" he told her. "Kitty is afraid we'll be keeping Mrs Mercer waiting. She says we can come back here when we leave the shop."

Sally went with him at once, though she knew she would never again see the old man making animals with plasticine. She had seen him. That was what mattered.

"It was foolish to come this way!" confessed Kitty when they came up to her. "We should have gone straight to the shop. Only I do love this market! The colours!"

"The shapes!" cried Sally.

Dominick pushed between them, catching their arms and pulling them forward.

"Aren't you girls lucky to have a brother to take care of you?" he demanded.

17
Mrs Mercer's Shop

hey jumped down steps, crossed a narrow street and went into another part of the market, where Dominick urged his sisters on so rapidly that people, whose heavy bags and baskets were being pushed this way and that, glared indignantly at the hurrying three.

Kitty stopped suddenly.

"Dom! You mustn't push like that! It's shocking manners!"

She turned to a young woman who was struggling with two little boys, a bulging shopping-bag and a tiny Christmas-tree.

"I'm terribly sorry, ma'am," she said. "I do hope we haven't hurt the little tree."

The woman smiled.

"Never mind, dear. I know what boys are.

Here am I landed with two of my own!"

They laughed but Dominick's face was crimson.

"Talks as if I'm a kid!" he muttered wrathfully.

They came out of the market and went to the right through almost deserted streets. As they waited with a mass of sightseers, shoppers, idlers, to cross the great curve of a road with even more dazzling shops than they had seen before, Sally became suddenly frightened.

"I don't want to see Mrs Mercer!" she declared.

Kitty and Dominick didn't hear her. They were too concerned with watching for their chance to cross and reach the far pavement.

The stream of buses, motors, lorries, cyclists came to a sudden stop as the red traffic lights flashed. The waiting crowd surged forward and there they were in a network of small streets, with elegant houses belonging to other days, friendly shops, hotels with courtyards and, still farther, a criss-cross of lanes where no heavy traffic could pass.

Here were shops like the small ones in Cork, leisurely people who studied brassware, pottery, books, pictures, china. There were shops with curtained windows where people sat drinking tea and eating cakes. A few of the shops even had little tables on the pavement outside, with gaily coloured check tablecloths, giving the place a Continental air.

"They say this is just like a village in the heart of London," said Kitty reflectively. "Here we are!"

Sally had been very impressed by the long, wide roads, the stately buildings, the beautiful shops like palaces. But now and again she had a longing for the tumbledown friendliness of Wise's Hill, the easy spaciousness of Patrick's Bridge and the endless variety of little shops along the quays.

She had thought Cork must be the largest city in the world. Now she was feeling glad it wasn't. Yet here, in the midst of this great city, was a quiet restful village which might have been dropped out of a fairy-tale.

They stopped outside a shop which would have been at home on Pope's Quay, with the Lee flowing gently past. Two steps led down to a closed door. The windows on either side had small panes, each with a blob of green glass in the middle, so that the treasures within flickered and gleamed as though they lay at the bottom of a restless sea.

In one window a small silver Christmas-tree,

with tiny coloured lanterns at the end of each branch, grew out of a heap of shining amethyst brooches, rings and buckles of beaten silver.

In the centre of the other window was a painting of a grey castle thrusting into a tossing river which sped inland towards a city with hills around like a protecting wall, rising up on three sides.

Winding roads climbed between tall houses to where grand mansions looked calmly down. The sky was heavy with grey clouds.

Sally cried out in delighted recognition.

"That's home! That's Cork! Oh, Kitty! That must be Wise's Hill!"

She turned to her sister who was gazing at the picture with wide open eyes and a smile on her lips.

"I remember when you painted that!" stammered Dominick. "But, Kitty! I can't have looked at it properly. I never knew it was so lovely!"

"Did you really paint that?" asked Sally, looking at Kitty in admiration.

"Of course she did," declared Dominick scornfully. "Can't you read? Look! *K. N.* down in the corner. Who else could have painted it? And look there! Don't ask who did that!"

He nodded at the dark brown figure of a

leprechaun leaning in the corner of the window.

Staring at it Sally could almost smell burnt dough.

"It's mine!" she cried.

The door was thrown open and a tall, thin woman with tumbled hair, a very long green necklace twisted round and round her neck, and hanging down the front of her black silk frock, smiled out at them.

"So here's the young genius!" she said in a quick, sharp voice which yet was friendly and welcoming. "Come in! Come in! So you were looking at Kitty's picture. Good, I think? Maybe you have an understanding of art, though you're still a child!"

She turned so suddenly that Sally tumbled down the steps, clutched at the carved arm of a high-backed wooden chair, dropped into it and gazed at Mrs Mercer in bewilderment.

"I like it!" she answered. "Though it makes me feel sad. I lived up there, on Wise's Hill, with the Mooneys. They went to America and Kitty brought me to London."

Mrs Mercer stood looking down at Sally, her hands on her hips, while Dominick squeezed in and Kitty closed the door gently.

"Do you hate London?" asked the tall, thin woman. "Are you afraid of it?"

"I don't hate it," answered Sally slowly. "But I am afraid of it!"

"So was I—once!" Mrs Mercer told her. "That was before I came here. Kitty feared this great city too, until I found her a refuge. Now, I think, she is happy. You are, aren't you?"

She looked suddenly at Kitty and the girl nodded.

"Thanks to you!" she replied, though her voice was uncertain.

"London is an amazing wilderness," continued the curio dealer. "People need a refuge here, more than they need a home. It isn't easy to make a home in a great city. But if you have a refuge you may find happiness.

"Many people find a refuge in their work. That is very good. It's a thrilling adventure to live in London, an adventure from dawn to dark, from one year's end to another."

"From Kitty's window you can see ships and masts and funnels," Sally informed Mrs Mercer. "There's a stone bridge and many strange people go across it. I never see them come back!"

She paused and went on speaking more to herself than to Mrs Mercer.

"Today I have seen wonderful shops, bigger and grander than any in Patrick Street. Only

London isn't all like that!"

She looked up as if waking from a dream.

"Go on!" ordered the thin woman, brushing back her thick red hair. "Tell me about London!"

Kitty frowned. Should she stop her sister? She knew Mrs Mercer loved this great city which had given her the opportunity to make the life she wanted. Would she resent Sally's talk?

But her young sister was talking away, gazing at the sharp-eyed shopkeeper with great friendliness.

"If London was all fine shops and splendid places to eat in, and picture galleries and parks and great buildings, I suppose it would be the best city in the world. But it isn't!"

Mrs Mercer stood listening and smiling. She glanced at Dominick and gave him a nod.

"I liked your leprechauns," she said, holding her chin in one thin hand as she gazed down at Sally. "I want you to do more. They're easy to sell. But to do better work you need teaching and training. I think you have real ability. But I know little of such things. I buy and sell objects of beauty. Yet I am ignorant of how most of them are made.

"It has taken me years to discover their real value. You are very young and I wouldn't want to put you on the wrong road. I've been finding out what you should do.

"You see that pile of forms and leaflets"—she pointed to a table littered with papers—"they are from various art schools. You will have to go to classes and I want to make sure you go to the best!"

She glanced at Kitty's anxious face.

"Don't worry, my dear," she said. "I know what I pay you, and you can't afford to pay for art classes as well as give the children a home. Besides, your work is good too. That picture has made me understand the kind of work you should be doing.

"I know that painting of Cork was done months ago and it was poked under a heap of old canvases. It took this child with her leprechaun of dough to wake me up and I put the picture and the figure in the window together."

Sally settled in the armchair and heard the talk going on. The carved knobs prodded her. But she didn't mind. The chair needed cushions to make it comfortable. She was sure that Kitty's pictures were lovely.

She felt she would not bother about hammering lumps of rock. She would get some soft clay and make the figures she liked—cats, dogs, horses, leprechauns, boys running, girls skipping.

Sally fell asleep.

She was awakened by someone thumping on the door. Mrs Mercer and Kitty were sitting on a chest still talking earnestly. At least Mrs Mercer was talking and Kitty listening. They were so absorbed in their talk that they didn't hear the knocks. Dominick tugged the door open.

A tall, bearded man in grey tweeds, holding a peaked cap in his hand, came down into the shop.

Mrs Mercer stopped talking. They all stared at the stranger, who came to a stop with his back to Sally and peered at Kitty with a puzzled shake of his head.

"Who are you—and where do you come from?" he demanded.

18
An Exile's Story

ho are *you* and what do you want? That's the question!" said Mrs Mercer, standing up to face him.

He looked not at her but at Kitty's dancing eyes and cloud of dark, silky hair.

"I am John Nolan from Cork City and I come seeking my family."

He spoke so gently that Kitty longed to fling her arms around him. She was sure he was her father, although the years had blotted him from her memory.

"He's the man we saw in the picture gallery!" thought Sally. "The man who was asking questions about us!"

Kitty stood still remembering the anguish and terror she had felt when her mother died and the letters written by her neighbours to her father remained unanswered.

Their friends on Wise's Hill had been sorry for the young orphans and when Kitty decided to go to London with Dom they had taken care of Sally.

It was long before she could forget her young sister's frightened face when they said goodbye in Cork. And she had a dread of this strange new big city where she had no friends.

Gradually she made a place for herself in London. Dominick went to school with the key of their room slung round his neck by a piece of tape. He was soon popular with the other boys, and while Kitty found it hard to conquer her fears, he became happy and confident.

Not until Kitty had found the curio shop and Mrs Mercer, did the girl feel she belonged to London. Her life in the past few years had been so full of new experiences and cares that she had almost forgotten her father as she thought he had forgotten her.

"Sit down!" said Mrs Mercer to the man. "If you are really the father of these children why did you leave them alone so long?"

The curio dealer was puzzled and indignant. She felt there must be some explanation. She could not believe this gentle, sorrowful man would abandon his wife and children.

"Someone is knocking at the door!" interrupted Dominick.

"Take your father to the inner room," Mrs Mercer told Kitty. "I will be with you as soon as I can."

The four trooped into a back room looking out on to a paved yard with trees in tubs and a green-painted garden seat. A cushioned settee was ranged opposite a blazing fire.

Kitty sat in the middle, Sally on one side, Dominick on the other. They stared nervously at the tall man who stretched himself in an armchair and smiled at them.

"I don't understand," he said softly as he looked at them. "When I left home there was a baby boy, a little girl and a bigger one. Now the baby seems to have turned into the girl. Is my mind still wandering?"

"It's Sally being so small has you mixed up," Dominick explained. "She's older than me but she's smaller. That's because I'm so big!"

He stood up to show his height and they all laughed.

"You're right there! I was mixed!" declared the man. "But now I must explain myself."

He sighed and Kitty began to feel sorry for him, though she could not forget her mother's loneliness and her own terror.

"When I went to America," began John Nolan, speaking as if he were feeling every word, "I meant to write each week, to send money and to bring you all out as soon as I could. I had letters to other Cork people who had emigrated, but before I could find any of them I was knocked down by a motor-car in New York as I was crossing the road.

"I was taken to hospital and was there for weeks. I was pretty badly knocked about but they made me well. My head had been injured, and though I grew strong I couldn't even remember my name. All my papers and belongings had been lost and I had to begin life again.

"If I had gone to the Irish Consul he might have been able to help me. I do not know. But the moment I was out of hospital I had to find work. I went from one big city to another and did any work that offered.

"At first I did hard, rough work, but then I became partner to a man who bought and sold. I became more prosperous. Yet I didn't even know my name. I called myself Gerald Griffin."

He paused and passed his hand over his head. He had four listeners now, for Mrs Mercer had come in from the shop. Their eyes were fixed on his face. No one moved. They scarcely breathed.

"One day," he resumed, "I had to sign an official paper. I did this in a hurry and suddenly I realized I had signed not Gerald Griffin but John Nolan!"

"Did they put you in prison?" asked Dominick in a whisper.

Mrs Mercer frowned at him. But the man sitting by the fire did not notice. He went on as if talking to himself.

"My memory began to come back. I felt that John Nolan was my rightful name and I had dim memories of Cork City. By this time I was doing well in business. I had good clothes, plenty of money and, best of all, I could go home.

"I did what I should have done at the beginning. I went to the Irish Consul. He did what he could. But the people he wrote to could find no trace of my family. I had left it too long!

"Taking his advice I booked a seat on a plane to the Shannon. When I arrived I spent a night in Limerick. I didn't have to explain myself. Every person I met knew I was a returned emigrant the moment I opened my mouth. That made me feel more of a stranger than ever. So I packed my bag and set off for Cork."

"Did you go in a train or a plane?" asked Dominick.

"A train," he replied. "Perhaps I didn't want

to arrive too quickly."

"Why?" said Dominick. "Didn't you want to go home?"

"Maybe I was afraid of what I'd find, or wouldn't find."

Mrs Mercer sighed.

"You found little of what you expected?" she asked.

"Hoped, not expected," he murmured. "I learned that my wife had died, that my elder girl and the boy had gone off to London and had come back for little Sally. I heard plenty about Sally. But no one knew where she was. The people she had been living with had emigrated to America. That was all I could discover. So I set off for London to continue my search."

"On a ship?" asked Dominick eagerly. "We came on the *Wave of Tory*."

His father chuckled.

"No, I flew! Suddenly ships and trains were too slow. I was sure I would find my children in London. But I did not realize how hard it was to search for them in a city of ten million people!"

"You did find us!" put in Kitty.

He nodded and continued his story.

"I went to all the Irish offices. They made inquiries and sent me from one to the other. I was impatient and explored London, always seeking. One day, by a fortunate chance, I went into a picture gallery and helped a boy who was mixed up with a revolving door."

He looked at Dominick and raised his eyebrows.

"It wasn't my fault," objected the boy. "It was some silly eejit who wanted to go the wrong way!"

"That lad's face," said the man, "reminded me of someone I had known. Before I could be sure he had disappeared. I spoke to an attendant who advised me to wait at the entrance. I waited but the crowd was too great and I couldn't catch a glimpse of him again."

"I saw you!" cried Sally triumphantly. "I thought you were looking at Kitty!"

Her father gazed through the window, remembering his search.

"I went to the Irish Club," he told them. "There I met a man who thought he knew you. He could not be sure because I could not describe you very well. But he gave me this address and said that Kitty worked here.

"When I found this place and saw the picture of Cork and the queer-looking leprechaun in the window I guessed I was on the right track."

"I'm glad you've found us after all these years!" said Kitty.

"Me too!" said Dominick.

"So am I!" added Sally.

"I must look after you now," said their father, "and we will forget the past and all its troubles."

Kitty looked at him gravely.

"I wouldn't want to do that!" she said.

He looked at his eldest daughter as if seeing her for the first time.

"You have a talented family," Mrs Mercer told him. "Kitty is the artist. Sally made the leprechaun."

Mr Nolan looked at Dominick.

"And you?" he asked. "What do you do, Dom? Are you a singer or a musician?"

Dominick grinned.

"I have my work cut out looking after the girls," he told his father.

19
Pictures in the Snow

rs Mercer closed the shop and they went out to lunch at a tiny restaurant round the corner.

They had a table in a square window where a fir-tree hung with glittering ornaments filled the space between the gay curtains. Few people went by and soon the children felt they were in a little house of their own. Kitty could hardly believe that her father was really there.

If they looked over their shoulders they could see people bending over piled plates, eating steadily and talking gaily. Sally preferred to watch the sparrows picking invisible crumbs from sheltered crevices between the paving-stones.

Kitty wished they had decorated their room in the Triangle. She had planned to have a

Christmas-tree, sprays of holly, a sprig of mistletoe, a tall red candle like they had in Cork.

John Nolan talked softly. Sally was too busy with her own thoughts and dreams to listen to him. He had been silent and lost among strangers for so long that he wanted to talk of his adventures. No one interrupted him but he stopped suddenly.

"My story can wait," he said. "Your future is more important than my past."

He turned to Mrs Mercer.

"What should I do first?" he asked her. "How can I make a home for my children?"

Mrs Mercer put her elbows on the table and clasped her hands beneath her chin.

"That depends on whether you decide to stay in London or return to Cork," she answered. "If I were in your place I would stay, for this is my world. Kitty has told me a lot about Cork. It must be a lovely place to live in. But so many have to leave it. Going back is never easy. Why not stay in London for the winter? You can take a trip to Cork in the spring. You will see the best of both cities and be able to choose."

She looked from one intent face to the other and smiled to herself.

"They are like all emigrants," she reflected.

"They dream of the day when they will return. Yet when the time comes they find it hard to go. New friends, new ambitions, a new way of life. All this makes it difficult. But they are still strangers in a strange land."

Kitty, staring beyond the little Christmas-tree, thought of the picture she had painted—Blackrock Castle, the tossing, silvery river, the magical city of Cork on its island. That was her dream. The reality had been a responsibility too heavy for her years, a loneliness which had never left her. If she went back now she wouldn't return to the knowledge that no one cared whether she came or went. She would have her father.

Dominick, eating strange dainties he hadn't known about before, smiled contentedly. Did it matter where you lived? Where there were people there would be friends. He knew Irish boys in London and he would know others in Cork.

A vision of flying between Cork and London flashed before his eyes. If Kitty stayed in London and his father went back to Cork he would go backwards and forwards. There was no need to give up anything or anybody. He took another spoonful of Christmas pudding and gazed out comfortably at the snowflakes which were drifting past the patch of light and disappearing.

Sally watched their flight too. But she saw Wise's Hill through the white drifting curtain. She knew her father would take them back if they wanted to go. Her friends the Mooneys were gone. But Janey might return.

The ballad singer she had known might even now be wandering up towards Monte Notte. The turf seller and his patient little donkey would be marching out of the city into the open country beyond.

She looked at her father. He had said he would give them everything they wanted. She knew what she longed for most—to mould with her fingers all the shapes that came into her mind.

She leaned back, her eyes dreamy and contented. Her father would decide what was best for them to do. If they stayed in London they would be together. If she went to Cork she could still do her work.

She had made friends in London. There was Marcella and her brothers. She would like them to know that she had found her father. Sally went on dreaming.

"I wonder what you are thinking about, Sally!" said her father, smiling at her. "Is it the

Christmas-tree, the pudding or the snow?"

How could she tell him? She gazed at him with her big solemn eyes. She knew that he wanted to give her and Kitty and Dominick all they had longed for. But most important of all he had given them a father.

Sally had always thought of home as a house with a garden, a mother, a father, a brother, a sister, a dog and a cat. For a little while she had had the brother and sister. Now she had a father. She couldn't remember her mother but soon she expected she would hear all about her.

Her father repeated his question and Kitty answered for her.

"I think she's like me—happy at having a father at last. You can tell us of the home we used to have in Cork. I've almost forgotten it. Sally and Dom can't remember what it was like—I'm sure of that!"

Her father laughed.

"I can see we'll never be dull. We have to share our past, present and future all at once. I've been planning a real Christmas. First we'll go to Midnight Mass at Westminster Cathedral on Christmas Eve. You'll spend Christmas Day with me at my hotel and I'll take you back to the Triangle.

"After Christmas we'll hold a Council of the

Future—your future and mine. Tomorrow I'll take you out to buy presents and you can help me choose one for Mrs Mercer."

He smiled at Mrs Mercer. She smiled back. She knew Kitty might not return to her after Christmas but they would always be friends.

Mr Nolan and Kitty, with Dominick's excited help, sat planning their Christmas. Sally leaned back in the shadowed corner, looking out beyond the Christmas-tree where the slanting snowflakes formed a background to her dreams.

She lived again that last evening on Wise's Hill, only now it was mingled with the first evening of her return.

"Of course I will go back," she reflected. "If I don't go now I'll go when I'm grown up. Janey and Des and Der will be coming out to meet me and they'll be grown up too. I wonder will Mr Mooney be there? I don't mind about him so much but I do want Mrs Mooney. I'd love her to see my new shoes and my best coat, for I must have grand clothes for the journey. And I'll make a lovely leprechaun specially for her."

"Sally!" said Kitty's laughing voice, interrupting her day-dream. "You never really told us all that happened after Dom came to London and before we brought you here. Now is your chance to tell it properly!"

Sally drew a deep breath.

"I was lonesome then but I'm not lonely now," she said. "There'll be time enough for all our stories when Christmas is over and we start our new life."